SPECIAL MESSAGE TO READERS

THE ULVERSCROFT FOUNDATION
(registered UK charity number 264873)

was established in 1972 to provide funds for
research, diagnosis and treatment of eye diseases.
Examples of major projects funded by
the Ulverscroft Foundation are:-

- The Children's Eye Unit at Moorfields Eye Hospital, London
- The Ulverscroft Children's Eye Unit at Great Ormond Street Hospital for Sick Children
- Funding research into eye diseases and treatment at the Department of Ophthalmology, University of Leicester
- The Ulverscroft Vision Research Group, Institute of Child Health
- Twin operating theatres at the Western Ophthalmic Hospital, London
- The Chair of Ophthalmology at the Royal Australian College of Ophthalmologists

You can help further the work of the Foundation
by making a donation or leaving a legacy.
Every contribution is gratefully received. If you
would like to help support the Foundation or
require further information, please contact:

THE ULVERSCROFT FOUNDATION
The Green, Bradgate Road, Anstey
Leicester LE7 7FU, England
Tel: (0116) 236 4325

website: www.foundation.ulverscroft.com

A FRENCH PIROUETTE

After an accident in rehearsals, Suzette, a famous French ballerina, disappears to an auberge in Brittany to recuperate. Libby, a young English widow, is starting a new life running the auberge, purchased from her old friend Odette. The summer is full of ups and downs for all three — Suzette meets Pascal, Libby turns the head of local vet Lucas, and Odette is thrilled when her pregnant daughter returns to Brittany — as they come to terms with the changes in their lives.

Books by Jennifer Bohnet
in the Linford Romance Library:

CALL OF THE SEA
WHERE THE SUN SHINES BRIGHTER

JENNIFER BOHNET

A FRENCH PIROUETTE

Complete and Unabridged

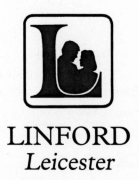

LINFORD
Leicester

First published in Great Britain in 2015

First Linford Edition
published 2015

A catalogue record for this book is available
from the British Library.

ISBN 978–1–4448–2441–4

Published by
F. A. Thorpe (Publishing)
Anstey, Leicestershire

Set by Words & Graphics Ltd.
Anstey, Leicestershire
Printed and bound in Great Britain by
T. J. International Ltd., Padstow, Cornwall

This book is printed on acid-free paper

1

Suzette

Suzette Shelby, the world-famous French ballerina, was soaking her feet in her Paris apartment; something she did routinely even when she was 'resting'. Ruefully, she lifted her feet out of the water and studied them.

Misshapen old lady's feet with bunions and callouses stuck on the end of her 38-year-old legs. Legs that were still shapely with the taut, muscled calves and thighs of a dancer. Picking up the soft-as-down large white towel she'd hung over the heated rail, she carefully wrapped her feet in it and gently began to pat them dry. The warmth cocooned her feet. Bliss.

The ballet company's official chiropodist was always stressing about her feet these days, but aside from emergencies she refused to let anybody touch them.

Removal of the callouses would only give her blisters. The bunions she'd deal with later when she retired.

Retired. A word that had entered her vocabulary in recent months and was threatening to take over her life. It would have to happen soon, she knew. She was lucky to have lasted at the top for so long. Many dancers were finished by their early 30s. Usually by then the injuries had mounted up and the RICE — rest, ice, compression, elevation — recovery times were lengthening.

Towelling her feet dry, Suzette grimaced. RICE. Such a funny expression for something that was as much a part of a dancer's life as barre work, while rice the food, with all its carbohydrates, was forbidden in her low-carb diet. It was a constant battle to keep fit and strong enough to dance but stay fat-free and trim.

The last three weeks had been a mixture of low-key exercises and RICE after that last sprain in Covent Garden. But now it was time to get back on the treadmill again: hours of gruelling dance practice, long rehearsals, and the need to network and help publicise the next show. The first of the publicity stints was starting with this afternoon's recording of a chat show at the TV studio.

Appearing on chat shows was not something that she did routinely, but Malik had assured her that a) these days keeping her name in front of her audience was essential and b) she might even enjoy it. It could even lead to other things when she retired. There was that word again. Retired.

She'd hoped that Malik would be back in Paris to escort her to the studios or at least meet her afterwards, but he was still down in Monaco. After tying things up there for the spring season he'd decided to stay on for a break. He'd asked her to join him but Suzette had said no, preferring to stay up here in town and get her ankle in tip-top condition before going down there to perform in a few weeks' time.

Malik had been her dance partner until five years ago when, after one injury too many, he retired and became a choreographer. His reputation these days was so good he could be selective and choose the ballet companies he wanted to work with. Suzette loved it when they worked together and was looking forward to their short season in Monaco.

She missed dancing with Malik. They'd fitted together so well; understood each other and picked up on each other's vibes while on stage. Since he'd retired from dancing she hadn't had a regular partner, dancing instead with one of the various top-flight male dancers contracted for the different ballets.

Away from the theatre, too, she and Malik enjoyed a deep personal friendship. At one time everyone had expected their friendship to develop into something more, but it had never gone beyond the special friendship stage. He was still her best friend in the dance world though. In all her worlds actually. Outside of dancing there were precious few people she could consider friends these days.

Sighing, she stood up and hung the towel on the heated rail to dry. Time to get dressed. The car the studio was sending for her would be here soon. Time to put on her public face and smile for the cameras.

The other guests were already enjoying wine and nibbles when Suzette was shown into the green room at the studios. She recognised a well-known actor and one of France's ageing rock-and-roll stars.

The other woman guest was a writer who, immediately after they were introduced, asked brusquely, 'Read my latest?'

Suzette shook her head. '*Désolé*. Murder mysteries aren't my scene. Prefer a romance. I'm sure it will do well though.' She smiled at the woman, who tutted at her words and turned away.

The show's format meant that each

guest was introduced individually, until all five of them were sitting around a table laden with finger food the guest chef of the day had been coerced into providing. Bottles of wine were passed freely around in an effort to create an atmosphere of friends at lunch chatting intimately and enjoying themselves.

Suzette had the actor on one side of her and a young wannabe star from a current talent show on the other. After initial hesitations, talk flowed between them as the experienced presenter drew them all into the conversation. It was when the subject of hobbies came up that Suzette found herself in the spotlight.

'Suzette, I know you are a keen photographer, but you are also a very gifted needlewoman and accomplished embroiderer. Tell us how you got into that,' the presenter said.

'Like all good things, I learnt it at my mother's knee,' Suzette said. 'I find it very relaxing and always have a piece in my dressing room to work on. It helps to pass the time when I'm not on stage.'

'You were born and grew up here in Paris, didn't you?'

'Yes, I grew up in Paris,' Suzette said, ignoring the first part of the question. 'I had a happy childhood here — although being at ballet school it was also a very disciplined life.' She went on to explain how her world had revolved around ballet since the age of nine. 'The discipline I learnt there is ingrained in me now.' She sighed. 'Sometimes I wish I could just be me.'

As she spoke she realised that maybe it was not the right thing to say on national TV.

'Of course I love what I do and hope to continue for some time yet,' she added quickly. 'I'm really looking forward to my season here in Paris in the autumn.' There. At least Malik would be pleased with her for getting their show mentioned. She was relieved when the presenter didn't press her on the subject of what 'being just me' would entail, and then five minutes later wound up 'lunch' and the show was over.

On the way home, Suzette sank back into the seat of the limousine and remembered the way the words about just being herself had come out without her thinking about it. But if — when — she retired and gave up her life of dance altogether, that was exactly what she could be. Herself. Would she survive without dance though?

Thank goodness it was only another couple of days before Malik would be back and she could talk to him. The one person left who knew her well — although even he, as close as they were, didn't know her secret.

★   ★   ★

Her local presse kiosk on the corner of two streets just yards from her apartment was busy the following morning when Suzette went to pick up the current issue of *La Monde*. A large photograph of the countryside on the side of the kiosk caught her attention as

8

she stood in the queue. '*Venez en Bretagne pour vos vacances.*'

She remembered her mother taking her to Brittany for a holiday once when she was nine. The countryside had been beautiful and she'd yearned to stay for longer, but at the end of the holiday she'd been dragged crying to the train station and they'd returned to Paris. Ballet school had taken over her life and her mother's finances and there had been no more holidays.

Since then, of course, she'd travelled all over the world but had never been back to Brittany. Maybe when she retired she'd take a holiday there and see if it was as beautiful as she remembered.

Back in the apartment, Suzette picked up the white velvet evening cape she was personalising with some delicate embroidery beadwork while she waited for Malik. It was his first evening back from the south of France and they were due to go to the theatre and have supper afterwards in one of their favourite bistros.

She glanced at her watch. Malik was typically late. She'd so wanted to talk to him before they left for the theatre, but that clearly wasn't going to be an option.

Half an hour later than she'd expected him, Malik let himself into the apartment. '*Désolé*,' he said. 'I forgot the time. That's looking good,' he said, moving closer. 'Stunning, in fact.'

'Thank you. I'm really pleased with it,' Suzette answered. 'I decided I needed a cover-up to go with that dress I wore for the Cannes Film Festival last year. The one with no back, remember?'

'The scarlet one that caused such a sensation?' Malik said, smiling. 'The one a certain film star was very jealous of?'

'That's the one,' Suzette said, carefully placing the material on the special cloth she kept to wrap her work in.

Malik bent over to take a closer look. 'It's beautiful,' he said, studying the intricate butterfly, vine and flower layout Suzette was painstakingly creating.

'It's meant to be a tribute to Lesage. I adore his designs. I hope to finish it in time for Monaco. Talking of Monaco, how did it go?'

Malik shrugged. 'I would prefer to be using the Princess Grace Theatre, but the Grimaldi Forum has everything we need.' He glanced at her feet. 'How's the ankle?'

'As good as it ever gets these days,' Suzette said, glancing at him. 'Can we talk? I need your advice.'

'Over supper,' Malik promised. 'But now we need to get to the Champs-Élysées or we will miss the first act.'

'And whose fault would that be?' Suzette gently grumbled at him.

After the performance, it was nearly eleven o'clock before they were shown to a secluded table in the bistro and she was able to begin to voice to Malik her worries and fears about what the future might hold for her.

'I can't believe I said that line about

just wanting to be me, on live TV,' she said. 'I mean, it's almost as bad as saying 'I want to be alone'. Which I don't,' she said, laughing at the absurdity of it. Malik, when she looked at him, wasn't laughing. 'It must be all this thinking about retiring getting to me.' She sighed. 'The truth, please, Malik. Do you think my inevitable retirement from dancing is getting ever closer?' she said as he poured their champagne.

Carefully he put the bottle in the ice bucket, handed her a glass, picked up his own and took a sip before answering her. 'You still dance beautifully and are rated as one of the top ballerinas in the world, but I think the injuries are mounting up, which will become more and more a problem for you.'

Suzette sighed and waited. He was confirming what she already knew deep down.

'After Monaco, the only date you have is the short season here in town with me for *Swan Lake* at the Paris Opera, no?'

Suzette nodded. 'Not even been asked to do *The Nutcracker* this Christmas.'

Malik reached across the table and took her hand in his. 'I think after Paris, *ma chérie*, you would be advised to think about taking a new direction. Perhaps teach? Choreography? *Non!* I forbid choreography.' He wagged a finger at her. 'I do not need the competition.'

'As if I would ever be as good as you,' Suzette said.

'Maybe I take you on as my assistant, that way you have a new career and I need not worry.'

Suzette shook her head at him before taking a sip of her champagne. 'So it seems *Swan Lake* will be my personal swan song. My life over.'

'*Non* — you will have a new beginning,' Malik said. 'Look at me. I thought it was the end of my world when I had to retire, but I'm fine. I love my new career. You will too.'

'Doing what, Malik? I honestly don't

think I want to go down the choreo-graphy route, not even as your assistant. And I'm not at all sure I've the patience for teaching. I still remember how horrible my friends and I were to our teachers.' She drained her champagne glass before continuing. 'As for dealing with all the pushy yummy mummies who are convinced their little darling is going to be the star of the decade . . . ' She shook her head. 'Couldn't do it.'

She watched as the waiter placed a salad niçoise in front of her and steak *frites* in front of Malik. 'That's another thing — one day I want to be able to eat what I fancy without worrying.'

'If it will make you feel better, have a *frite*,' Malik said, piercing one onto his fork and holding it out.

'Thank you.' Suzette chewed the *frite* slowly, making it last. 'Life would be a lot simpler if only I had a family and a patient husband waiting in the wings to whisk me away to live a normal life.'

'Pshaw!' Malik said. 'Who wants a normal life, anyway? It would be boring. Something will turn up, you'll see. Paris is months away yet. You've got plenty of time to think and make decisions.'

Bleakly, Suzette smiled at him. The trouble was, she realised with a pang, she was starting to yearn desperately for a husband and a normal family life — always had, really — but dancing had taken precedence over everything. 'Have you truly never wanted to marry? Have a family?' she asked.

Malik shook his head. 'Never been high on my agenda, no. I've told you before, my home life wasn't that great. I didn't see the need to recreate a stressful situation that I was happier without. But then, unlike you, I don't have a biological clock ticking away.'

'No, you don't,' Suzette said. 'And you have at least been true to yourself. Whereas I . . . ' She paused. 'I have danced my life away, never really listening to the ticking of that clock. Perhaps retiring at the end of the year will be a good thing. I'll certainly have time to listen to — and maybe, if it's not too late — do something about the ticking.' She'd certainly have all the time in the world to just be herself, whether she liked it or not.

She sighed. It was just that the word 'retirement' made her feel so old. So past it.

★   ★   ★

'OK, guys. Let's take a short break. Back in fifteen,' Malik said. Suzette, along with the rest of the dancers, breathed a sigh of gratitude.

The company had arrived in Monaco three days ago — three days which had been filled with rehearsals and little else. Today was the final one before the dress rehearsal tomorrow. Opening night would be Friday with Prince Albert and Princess Charlene in the audience.

Back in her dressing room in the Grimaldi Forum, Suzette poured herself some water and did a few stretching exercises to keep herself limbered up.

Although initially she'd found Malik's choreography challenging, she was enjoying dancing this modern ballet now she'd finally broken through and mastered its intricacies. Her partner Zac, a young and up-and-coming Russian, was good and Suzette had rapidly felt confident in their on-stage chemistry.

There was a discrete knock on the door before Malik entered. He'd always been considerate, never assuming he could just barge in on her.

'You ready for the last scene in Act Three?'

Suzette nodded. It was a long, complicated piece with her doing several grand jetés in mid-air before an emotional dance with Zac, which involved her jumping into his arms.

'Think so. Bit worried about doing the splits in mid-air, actually,' she said. 'My dancing repertoire hasn't featured them much recently.'

'Relax. You mastered them fine yesterday,' Malik assured her.

Back down in the theatre, Suzette

went through her pre-dance stretching exercises while Malik put the corps de ballet through their routine. Standing in the wings waiting for her introductory music to play, Suzette felt the shiver of nervous anticipation she always experienced before she danced on stage. This was what she lived for.

Zac, in the opposite wing, smiled across at her before striding onto the stage ready for the first of their pas de deux. Five seconds later Suzette joined him and their bodies synchronised together in the flowing ballet movements. Everything else faded away as they lost themselves in the evocative music.

Suzette executed a final perfect allégro when disaster struck. Landing badly, she end up in a crumpled heap on the wooden stage.

'Stop the music!' Malik shouted as he rushed to her side. 'Get the doctor.'

'No,' Suzette said. 'I don't need the doctor. I'll be fine. Just give me ten minutes and a cold compress. Help me up please?' She held out a hand to Malik.

Even as Malik gently pulled her onto her feet before placing an arm around her shoulders to steady her before helping her off stage, Suzette knew she was in trouble. Real trouble. Experience told her that this injury was not going to heal quickly.

After the cold compress had been applied, Malik insisted she take a cab back to the hotel. 'You know it is impossible for you to dance again today, Suzette. Maybe with twenty-four hours' rest and ice.' He shrugged. 'We'll see.' Suzette could tell he was already mentally assessing the options he had.

Once back in her hotel room, Suzette gave way to the tears that had been threatening from the second she'd fallen. She knew that final jump had been perfect. How could she have been so stupid as to mess up the landing, and ruin everything? Thank heavens it hadn't happened on opening night in front of Prince Albert and Princess Charlene.

Her shame would have been absolute.

Malik returned in the early evening and insisted she order some food from room service, then opened the bottle of champagne he'd brought with him.

'I'm hardly celebrating,' Suzette snapped at him.

'This is medicinal champagne to make you feel better,' Malik answered, handing her a glass.

As she picked at the smoked salmon and salad she'd ordered, Malik said, 'I can't stay long. Suzette . . . ' He hesitated before continuing. 'I'm sorry about this, but I've had to give the role to Donna. She's rehearsing right now with Zac. I have to get back down there.'

'Every understudy's dream,' Suzette said. 'The show must go on.' She pushed her meal away. 'I could be back before the show ends. A couple of days and my ankle could be strong enough to dance.' Even as she said it, she knew she was lying to herself as well as Malik. This injury would take weeks rather than days to heal, which meant yet more RICE time before battling her body back into dancing fitness. There was no point either in telling Malik about her bruised and sore arm, which in its own way was as bad as her ankle and would make any port de bras movements difficult for weeks to come.

Malik shook his head. 'I can't take the risk.'

'No, I suppose not.' Suzette sighed, facing up to the inevitable. 'Wish Donna luck from me. You'd better get back down to the rehearsal.'

'You've got everything you need?' Malik said, clearly relieved she'd taken the news so well.

Suzette nodded. Of course she had everything she needed, except a functioning ankle. Her arm felt badly bruised too. No doubt it would be a mass of interesting colours by the morning.

As Malik closed the door behind him, Suzette downed her glass of champagne and immediately poured herself another one. It was one way to drown both the physical and the mental pain. Besides,

Malik had said it was medicinal.

Collapsing onto the bed, she switched on the TV and began to flick through the channels. Football, quiz games, reality shows, talk . . . Hang on, that was the show she'd recorded weeks ago. She recognised the woman crime-writer. The camera moved around the various guests and Suzette saw herself on screen, and watched herself utter the words, 'Sometimes I wish I could just be me.'

Thoughtfully, Suzette muted the TV sound. Had this latest accident just granted her unacknowledged wish? She looked down at her legs. Her knee was showing signs of a big colourful bruise while her ankle was two or three times its normal size. Suzette sighed. She'd been here so many times in the last few years.

But with the understudy now dancing in her place, she didn't have to try and rush getting fit. This Monaco show had been her only engagement of the year until Malik's Paris show in the autumn. Malik.

Would he still want her to dance in view of this recent catastrophe? Would he take the risk with her again? He'd already agreed with her that *Swan Lake* in Paris would probably be her own swan song from the world of ballet. She couldn't bear it if he cancelled her contract saying she wasn't fit enough to dance, thus denying her a final performance and all the accolades usually given to a retiring dancer.

Suzette straightened her shoulders. There was a whole summer before then — more than enough time to recuperate from these injuries and get completely fit again.

Carefully she stood up and reached for the walking stick that someone in the theatre had handed her as she left. Leaning heavily on it, she made her way across the room and picking up the phone asked for room service. 'I will need some help tomorrow morning please,' she said. 'About ten o'clock? Thank you.'

Thoughtfully replacing the receiver,

Suzette began to make plans for the following day. Malik would be busy giving Donna extra coaching, and then there was the dress rehearsal in the afternoon, so she doubted she'd see him before dinner tomorrow evening. A fact which suited her well in view of the decision she'd just come to. She sat down at the small desk, found a pen and took a piece of the hotel stationery.

'Darling Malik, I felt it best if I left. Hope the show is a huge success. See you in Paris. Love, Suzette.'

She'd ask reception to give it to him tomorrow evening when he returned. She knew if she stayed and told him personally, he would try to persuade her otherwise. It was best if she just left Monaco and disappeared.

2

Libby

Discovering the photos of their last holiday, as she searched for something in the miscellaneous drawer of the kitchen dresser, brought the memories flooding back for Libby Duncan. For years she and Dan had holidayed in France, staying at the Auberge du Canal in Brittany. Thoughtfully, she laid the photos on the table one by one. That holiday three years ago had been one of their best. Dan had been so full of plans for their future.

They'd often talked about moving to France. Dreamed about running a B&B, a gîte, enjoying the Good Life. But somehow something had always stopped them from taking the plunge. First it was Chloe's schooling; it was never a convenient time for her to change schools. Then it was Dan's job. A promotion meant more money but less time. Then it was Harriet, Ellie's mum, needing help after a hip replacement.

But on that last holiday Dan had insisted they start visiting the local immobiliers, looking for their dream home. 'We've got to do it soon, Libby, otherwise we'll be stuck in a rut forever.'

Their dreams had been cruelly shattered just two months later when Dan died. Dead from a heart attack at 46. Stress, the doctor had said.

Libby and Chloe had clung together and got through the awful time. Now here she was, preparing to face empty-nest syndrome while Chloe was getting ready for a fun gap year before she went off to college.

Libby knew that, unlike some widows, she was lucky to be financially secure — Dan had been well insured — but with Chloe growing up and becoming independent, she was beginning to feel it was time to get her own life back on a course she was happy with. Maybe it was time to sell the house? A new start in a new place. The only problem being she didn't have a clue as to which direction she wanted the rest of her life to go.

She picked up a photo of the auberge showing Dan sitting under the jasmine-covered loggia, raising a cool glass of rosé, a happy smile on his face. Libby could smell the sweet night air, hear the last of the daytime bees buzzing in the honeysuckle, and see the swallows swooping around as Dan savoured the tranquility of the summer evening.

Outside, the reality of January rain hammered at the windows. Snow had been forecast for the end of the week. Summer seemed a long way off.

Thoughtfully, Libby put the photo down on the table. Maybe she'd book a holiday for later in the year. It would be something to look forward to. A week at the Auberge du Canal with Odette and Bruno would be a wonderful antidote to winter — and maybe even help her to kick-start her life again.

She and Dan had become friendly with Odette and Bruno the very first time they'd stayed with them at the auberge. It was a friendship that had flourished over the generation gap from the moment they'd met and with two or three visits a year, Odette and Bruno were more like elderly family relatives now. They'd even crossed the channel and stayed with Libby and Dan here in Bath.

Odette had written her a lovely letter when she'd heard about Dan, telling her any time she felt the need to get away she knew she was more than welcome to stay with them. It was an offer Libby had so far failed to take up. Maybe now was the time?

There was a group photo of the four of them taken on a day out exploring the gardens of a restored château. Libby felt a pang of guilt. She hadn't spoken to Odette since Christmas. Tonight she'd put that right and ring. Wish her Happy New Year. It wasn't too late to do that the second week in

January. French people wished each other *bonne année* all through the month.

At the same time, she'd ask Odette about going to stay with them later in the year. Book the gîte next to the auberge for a fortnight's holiday for her and Chloe. When should they go? Oh, June. June was always a lovely month in Brittany. It would be something to finally look forward to.

Libby crossed to the phone. Why wait until this evening? Having made the decision, she wanted to get it organised. She'd phone now.

The phone rang and rang. Libby pictured the noise ringing around the large old-fashioned auberge kitchen where Odette spent most of her day preparing delicious meals. In the off season, even though there were few guests staying, the locals continued to use the restaurant, especially at weekends.

Libby was about to hang up, thinking Odette was too busy to answer, when a quiet voice in her ear said, '*Bonjour. Qui?*'

'Odette. It's Libby here. A bit late I know, but *bonne année. Comment allez-vous?*'

A slight pause. '*Ça va, merci, Libby. Bonne année à vous aussi.*'

Libby, sensing something wasn't right, said, 'Odette, what's wrong?'

'Bruno. He has broken the arm.'

'The arm? Oh, you mean his arm! Oh poor Bruno. Which one? Not his right one?'

'No, the wrong one.'

Libby struggled not to laugh at Odette's misunderstanding. 'His left arm then? *Gauche?*'

'*Oui.* And he drives me mad with his demands. All day he is wanting me to help him. I have ten people to dinner this evening and he wants me to help him in the garden.'

'How did he break it?'

'He fell off the ladder helping me decorate one of the *chambres*. So *naturellement*, he blames me!' Odette said, sighing. 'And you? How are you?'

'Chloe and I are fine, thank you.

Thinking of coming for a holiday this year if you have room for us?'

'Always, Libby, but there is *un petit problème,*' Odette said. 'The Auberge du Canal will be up for sale soon. Bruno's accident made him cross so now he decides to sell. We go to live in his mother's old house in the village.'

Libby remembered visiting the imposing Maison de Maître in the middle of the village with Odette. With its wrought-iron railings and large double gates separating it from the main village street, the tall detached house had clearly been built by someone of importance in an earlier age.

'You are welcome to stay with us there, Libby, if we have moved. It has enough rooms. When is it you wish to come?'

'June?'

'A good month. Let me know the dates later. Now, I have to go. Bruno is yelling for me.'

'OK. I'll phone you again. Bye.'

Libby replaced the receiver and moved across to the table. She picked up a photograph of the auberge and studied it. A crazy idea formed in her mind. An impossible idea. Wasn't it?

* ★ ★

Later that evening Chloe picked up the photographs Libby had left on the table and flicked through them. 'Dad was so happy on that holiday,' she said.

'He was,' Libby agreed. 'He adored the process of visiting immobiliers and looking at property. I know he felt his dream seemed to be finally coming within his grasp.'

They were both silent for several seconds before Libby spoke. 'I rang Odette earlier. They're selling the auberge.'

'What? Oh, it won't be the same without Odette and Bruno there when we go again.'

'You'd like to go again?'

Chloe nodded. 'Yes. I loved it there. I miss not going.'

'Chloe?'

'Mmm?'

'When Odette told me they were selling, I had this crazy idea that I might buy it,' Libby said. 'Of course I won't,' she added quickly. 'It's a stupid idea, really. Not worth thinking about.' She began to gather the photographs into a pile.

'No it's not. I think it's a brilliant idea.'

Libby stopped and looked at Chloe. 'You do? It would mean selling this house for a start.'

'It'll be a bit big for you anyway when I leave,' Chloe said practically. 'You'll need to downsize.'

'The auberge is bigger! And there's a gîte.'

'Yes, but it would be a business. You love having people to stay, fussing after them and cooking.'

'I so don't fuss!'

'You do, but in the nicest possible way,' Chloe said. 'I definitely think you should think about it seriously.'

'Really? You don't think it's too big a risk at my age, on my own?'

'Mum. You're not exactly on the scrap-heap yet. OK, I know you've got the big four-oh coming up this year but you're still in reasonable shape for an oldie.'

'Oldie?' Libby said. 'I'm not old. Besides, forty is the new thirty.'

'You will be old if you don't start living again. I know you miss Dad,' Chloe said. 'I do too. But you need to do something with your life. Besides, you might meet a sexy Frenchman. Get married again.'

Libby shook her head. Privately she'd accepted she'd struggle to replace what she and Dan had shared and had resigned herself to living life as a widow. She did need to do something with her life, though; Chloe was right about that.

Chloe looked at the photo of the auberge again. 'I could move over with you for a couple of months before I go to uni. Help you settle in.'

Libby held out her hand for the photo. 'With an offer like that, how can I hesitate? I'll ring Odette again and ask how much they want for the place. For all I know the price may be more than I can afford anyway.'

For the next few days Libby thought about the wisdom of moving to France on her own. Because she would be on her own once Chloe had started her course and was back in England. Holidays in a foreign country were one thing; moving there permanently on her own was totally different.

Holidays at the auberge had been wonderful. Libby thoughtfully fingered the photographs she'd been unable to put away, remembering how idyllic it had always been. The way they'd dreamt of moving to France; of changing their lives.

Could she resurrect the dream? Do it on her own?

She'd agonised for days over what to do. So many questions and what-ifs had tumbled around in her head. As Chloe had so kindly pointed out, she had a big birthday coming up, but hopefully she still had a lot of years ahead of her. She had to do something, and working at something she enjoyed would be better than doing any old thing. But could she resurrect the dream by herself, for herself? She'd always liked having relatives and friends to stay. Loved cooking special meals for them. Was it up to French standards though? Was her French up to coping?

It was remembering Dan describing how he longed to get out of the rut they were in that decided her. The rut could only get deeper as the years went by.

Odette, when Libby rang her Sunday morning, was thrilled at the thought of Libby buying the auberge. 'You would be perfect. I do want it to go to someone I like,' she said. 'It will be hard for you alone but I will 'elp you all I can.'

The price, when Odette told her, took Libby's breath away in surprise. Affording it would not be a problem after all. She'd forgotten how reasonable property still was in Brittany. Dan's insurance money and the money from the sale of the house would cover it.

Libby took a deep breath. She'd be brave and do it. Use Dan's money to fulfil his dream for both of them.

'I'll have to sell here, Odette. But yes, I would like to buy the Auberge du Canal.'

It was surprising how fast things happened after the decision had been made. Libby decided against going to Brittany to view the auberge, feeling that she knew it well enough already. It wasn't as if she was buying something unknown.

Odette and Bruno agreed to her paying a large deposit and the rest when the house was sold. Various official papers passed from France to England and back again, usually in triplicate and signed and initialed in several places. Odette and Bruno said Libby should move in as soon as possible to keep the continuity of the business going.

The house was put on the market and Libby started a month of frantic de-cluttering and packing. Chloe helped and between them they decided on the various bits and pieces Libby should take to France.

Furniture was easy. The auberge was coming fully furnished, apart from the two-bedroom owner's apartment. So the beds and other furniture from both their bedrooms would be needed, as would the sitting-room furniture.

It was the personal items that caused the most problems. Paintings, ornaments and books. What to keep and what to take to the local charity shops? Many of the books had been Dan's on such diverse subjects as fishing, car mechanics, physics and his well-read Wilbur Smiths. Chloe made what she called 'an executive decision' and took all of Dan's books, except the Wilbur Smiths, down to the Oxfam shop in the high street. 'You can put everything else in the sitting room of the auberge,' she said.

In between the de-cluttering and the packing, they had several couples view the house before an acceptable offer was made. From then on, the pace of urgent things to do sped up. In the end, it was just eight weeks from deciding to buy the Auberge du Canal, to Libby finding herself boarding the ferry with her remaining worldly goods on her way to a new life in France.

★　★　★

The sound of rushing water woke Libby. It was several seconds before she remembered where she was. As realisation dawned, she smiled happily.

She'd done it. She and Chloe were actually in France.

Last night she'd deliberately opened the bedroom window slightly before closing the shutters, so that as she collapsed exhausted into bed the noise of the canal would lull her to sleep. Laying in bed at either end of the day listening to the water's rhythmic movement had always been a special part of past holidays. Now it was about to become a part of her future daily routine.

Stretching out her hand, Libby picked up the silver-framed photograph she'd placed on the floor beside the bed last night. Gently she stroked the glass. 'Wish you were here with me, Dan,' she said softly.

This photo of Dan sitting outside on the terrace by the canal evoked so many wonderful holiday memories. Evening walks along the canal path with the swallows swooping around their heads. Supper on the terrace overlooking the canal. Watching the occasional boat manoeuvre its way through the lock, making its way to a mooring alongside the village quay. The wonderful meals Odette had made for them. Their dream of living the Good Life.

And now here she was, planning to do it all on her own. Libby brushed a tear away.

Since the decision had been made and everything had snowballed into place, she'd been outwardly buoyed up with enthusiasm, but at the same time she was secretly terrified at what she had set in motion. When Helen, Dan's sister and Chloe's godmother, had voiced her concern, Libby did try to explain her feelings.

'It's such a big step, Libby. I know it was always a dream of yours and Dan's to do this together — but on your own?' And Helen had shaken her head.

'I know,' Libby said. 'But I have to do something and I'm a big girl now; I'm sure I'll cope on my own. Chloe will be there for the summer too, don't forget.' She'd smiled reassuringly. When Helen failed to look convinced, she added, 'Helen, please don't worry. I can't tell you how energised I feel about this move. After the last couple of years, I feel like I'm waking up again. I'm ninety-nine percent certain I'm doing the right thing. If I'm not, and it all goes wrong, I can always sell up and come home, but at least I'll have tried to do something with my life.'

'Well, I wish you all the luck in the

world,' Helen said. 'Can I come and visit?'

'Of course. Give me a week or two to settle in and you'll be more than welcome.'

Now, alone in the auberge bedroom which she and Dan had occupied together so often, she could only pray that she'd done the right thing coming to France on her own. Thoughtfully Libby put Dan's photograph back down on the floor. 'I'll make our dream come true,' she whispered.

'Morning, Mum.' Chloe pushed open the bedroom door with her foot. 'Brought you breakfast,' she said, carefully placing a tray on the bed.

'Goodness,' Libby said, looking at the fresh croissants on the tray. 'You're up and about early.'

'Did my run to the village.' Chloe grinned. 'Where the boulangerie just happened to be open. So I've earned my *pain au chocolat*. You'll have to work yours off later!'

'That won't be hard,' Libby said,

'with this place to be sorted. Lots of unpacking to do today. Mmm, I'd forgotten how good these are,' she added, dunking her pain au chocolate in the bowl of coffee in true French style.

The sudden noisy crowing of a cockerel startled them. 'Napoleon,' Chloe said. 'Wants his breakfast.'

Libby looked at her blankly.

'You remember, Mum. Odette told you she was leaving the hens and ducks for you. Napoleon the cockerel comes with them. I'll go and feed them if you like, while you shower.'

'Thanks.'

Libby sighed as Chloe left the room. She was going to miss having her around so much when she left for college, leaving her to live alone for the first time ever. Running her shower and standing under the hot, invigorating water, Libby pushed all thoughts of Chloe leaving away. She wouldn't start worrying about it now. There was a whole summer to enjoy before she left.

'Mum! Come here quickly.' Chloe's

urgent shout broke into her thoughts as she towelled herself dry. Quickly she pulled on some clothes and ran downstairs.

'Whatever is the matter . . . ?' she asked, her voice trailing away as she saw exactly what the matter was. The kitchen was flooded and water was pouring out through the back door and down the steps.

'Thought I'd put some washing on but the machine won't stop taking in water,' Chloe said. 'Even though I've turned it off.'

'We need to turn off the stopcock,' Libby said. 'And I have no idea where that is. I'll phone Odette. But first I'll turn the electricity off at the mains — I think the switch for that is in this cupboard by the door. Yes!' She pushed the big switch on the right down to the 'off' position.

Picking up the phone, she dialled Odette's number. Quickly explaining the situation, she listened intently as Odette told her where the stopcock was.

'Outside by the gîte. I send Bruno to help you. He knows what to do.'

Running outside, Libby found the stopcock under a large metal cover and turned the water off. By the time Bruno arrived carrying his bag of tools, she and Chloe were busy mopping up the water in the kitchen.

Bruno dragged the machine out to reach the pipes behind and pulled out a piece of perished rubber hose. 'The machine is old. It happens occasionally,' he said. 'I fix it for now but a new machine might be better.'

'Thanks, Bruno,' Libby said. It looked like her shopping list had just got even longer.

Once Bruno had left and she'd tentatively switched everything back on with no mishaps, Libby breathed a sigh of relief. First crisis over. 'Everybody knows things go wrong when they move,' she said philosophically as she and Chloe began the final clean-up. 'Could be worse.'

For the next few days Libby and Chloe were busy sorting out the auberge. Together they inspected the whole place, with Libby making notes about everything she would need to buy. She was determined to give it a twenty-first-century makeover, change the slightly old-fashioned style of the place, and put her own mark on it, all without upsetting Odette.

Six double bedrooms, sitting room, dining room, cloakroom, and the kitchen. The bedrooms were all pretty much as Libby remembered them. Heavy Bretagne beds, four-drawer chests with a mirror placed above each, wardrobes to match the carved wooden bed-ends, and en-suite salle de bains. Even with the large furniture, the rooms were still spacious with plenty of room to add a comfortable chair or two — cane Lloyd Loom ones if she could find some. Also some bedside tables. For some reason Odette had never considered it necessary to supply those. Or tea- and coffee-making trays.

Odette had always insisted that guests were free to use the kitchen and didn't need to make drinks in their rooms. Libby had often wished she could make herself a warm drink, though, when she'd woken at 3 a.m. and didn't fancy trekking downstairs to the kitchen. Bedside tables with lights and a tray with tea-making facilities were essentials in her book.

'Love the white bed linen, Mum, but blankets?' Chloe said, opening the large armoire on the first-floor landing where all the bed linen was stored. 'Mmm, smell that lavender.'

'Definitely replace with duvets,' Libby said, scribbling a note. 'Some toile de Jouy covers and pillowcases would be pretty. Need some more white bath towels too.'

Some of the rooms could also do with decorating, she decided. Nothing much, just a lick of paint on the walls to freshen things up before the season began. Next winter would be the time to tackle any major decorating. The first guests were booked in for three weeks' time, so no time to do them all. She'd tackle the three on the first floor first. Large tins of paint went on the list.

'Now for my apartment,' Libby said as they climbed the final flight of stairs to the top floor and opened the apartment door with its private 'interdit' sign. 'It's going to feel funny living up here on my own,' she said, glancing at Chloe. 'D'you realise I've never lived on my own before?'

'Mum, stop worrying. It's going to be fine,' Chloe reassured her.

The couple of occasions in the past when Odette had invited them upstairs, Libby remembered the sitting room being small and full of large old-fashioned furniture. Now with her own furniture left higgledy-piggledy by the removal men, waiting for her to decide where to place it all, the room seemed bigger; full of possibilities. There was even a little balcony with room for one of those snazzy wrought-iron round tables and a chair. A perfect place to unwind in the evening, overlooking the canal and the woods on the opposite side.

Her bedroom, too, was a good size — big enough for the king-sized bed and the various other pieces she'd brought with her. She smiled ruefully, looking at the unmade bed with boxes of clothes dumped on it. Really she should have left it behind in the UK and bought a new, smaller one in France. But it was so comfortable, and she'd got used to having the luxury of so much space.

'Right, you ready to hit the shops?' Chloe asked, looking at the list in Libby's hand.

'I was going to check out the gîte as well,' Libby said. 'See what's needed in there. But that can wait for another day. Let's go.'

Three hours later Libby called a halt to the shopping, feeling that her bank account had been hit hard enough for one day. 'Think that's it for today. Don't think the car will hold another thing,' she said. 'Time to go home and get to work.'

Turning off the main road onto the narrow canal path with the car filled to the roof with boxes and bags, Libby slowed down to a crawl to avoid the pot-holes. The last thing she needed was to damage her car.

'At least we're not likely to meet anything, thank goodness. There's so much stuff in the car I couldn't possibly see to reverse,' she said.

'Umm, think you've spoken too soon,' Chloe said, indicating a dirty blue estate car in the distance moving at a fair speed towards them.

'Damn,' Libby muttered. 'D'you think they know I've just passed a lay-by? I'm going to keep going; I can't see to reverse properly. I'm sure there's another passing place further on. Hopefully they won't mind reversing.'

As she continued to edge slowly towards the other car, Libby was relieved to see it finally stop and then begin to go backwards quickly. The sun shining on the windscreen of the other car made it impossible to see who was driving other than that it appeared to be a man.

Thirty seconds later, as she drew alongside to pass, Libby raised her hand in acknowledgement and Chloe wound the window down to say thanks.

'If you're going to live here you need to learn to reverse,' the man said, wagging a finger at them. 'See you soon.' With that he was gone, churning up the road dust in his wake and leaving Libby and Chloe looking at each other.

'Bit rude,' Libby said. 'I'm quite capable of reversing normally.'

'Wonder who he is?' Chloe said. 'He was quite dishy in a laid-back, scruffy French way. Wonder what he meant by 'see you soon'?'

Libby shrugged as she pulled into the parking space outside the auberge. 'No idea. Can you take this box inside, please — needs to go in the sitting room. I'll bring the first of the duvets and then I'm going to put the kettle on. I need tea after all that shopping.'

They were sitting in the kitchen,

drinking tea and making plans to start on the unpacking and sorting things out, when Odette arrived.

'I thought I'd pop in to see how you were after the flood,' Odette said. 'And to offer to give you a hand Saturday.'

'Saturday?' Libby asked, pouring a cup of tea and handing it to Odette.

'The rally tea.'

Puzzled, Libby looked at her.

'The local vintage car club. Bruno's a member and we've always had the season's opening rally start and finish from here. It is in the reservations book,' Odette said.

'I haven't opened that book,' Libby said. 'In fact I'm not even sure where it is. I'd assumed the booking for three people at the end of the month was the first date I had to worry about.' She looked at Odette. 'How many people come on this rally? What kind of food do they want?' She shook her head. 'I'm not sure . . . '

'It's just sandwiches, cakes and tea. If it's cold, a bowl of soup is welcome,'

Odette said. 'I think last year there were thirty people.'

'Thirty! No, I can't possibly. Who's the organiser? I'll ring tonight and cancel. I'm sure they can find somewhere else when I explain I've only just moved in.'

'*Mais* Libby, it's not a problem with me to help this year,' Odette protested. She hesitated. 'I have told Lucas earlier that it will be OK.'

'Lucas?'

'Lucas Berrien; he is the organiser. When he called to see me earlier I promised him there was no problem with you because I would help. He said he'd driven down here to see you but then he got an emergency call so he had to leave.'

'Emergency? Who is he?'

'He's the local vetinaire,' Odette replied.

'What kind of car does he have?' Chloe asked.

'He has a vintage Delage that is the envy of all, but for his work he drives — '

'A muddy blue estate,' Libby finished the sentence for her.

'*Oui*. You've met him?'

'Only in passing,' Libby said.

'So that's why he said 'see you soon',' Chloe laughed. 'Go on, Mum. You can do it. Think of catering for the rally as your first challenge in France.'

'The rally will have to be stopped if you cancel the tea. It would be impossible to find somewhere else local at such short notice,' Odette said. 'Please, Libby. I promise you it is not difficult.'

Libby sighed. 'I don't suppose I have much choice really.' She looked at Odette. 'OK. You'd better fill me in with all the details — times, kinds of food and so on, and we'll work out a plan of action.' Talk about being thrown in at the deep end. But at least she'd have Odette and Chloe to help.

3

Odette

Standing in the sitting room of the old mas in the centre of the village, Odette determinedly rubbed her eyes in an effort to keep the tears she could feel threatening from running down her cheeks.

Bruno might be full of enthusiasm about moving back into the house where he was born, but it was the auberge that had meant everything to her. She knew living in the Maison de Maître in the village would not be the same. Of course she realised things changed and nothing stayed the same forever. She also knew the auberge had been getting not too much for her as Bruno insisted, but more old-fashioned and in need of updating. Something she'd hoped Bruno would help her do when he retired, but instead after his broken arm he'd said he wanted more time for them to do things together and insisted on putting the auberge up for sale.

'We haven't had a proper *vacances* in twenty years,' he said.

'We've been to Paris and Venice, several times,' Odette had protested. 'And London, Barcelona . . . We even got to Amsterdam.'

'They were just long weekends, and mainly out of season,' Bruno had said, dismissing them almost as non-events. 'I want a proper holiday, not something snatched between bookings.' He glanced at her before adding, 'I'm sure you'd like to spend time with Isabelle, too, down on the Riviera.'

She hadn't been able to argue with that. She'd missed Isabelle when she'd married and gone to live down south, with infrequent visits back home because of a busy work schedule. So she'd half-heartedly agreed that they'd sell the auberge, secretly planning to delay it as long as possible. Libby ringing up and saying she wanted to buy the place was something she'd not anticipated.

Odette did genuinely try and point out to Libby how hard she'd find it on her own, but Libby was adamant, saying she was doing it for Dan, and that it would do her good to have something to focus on. In the end Odette gave up and accepted the inevitable changes to her own life she seemed powerless to stop.

Crossing over to the window, Odette looked out over the village street. After just two days she missed the view and the noise of the canal water whooshing over the weir. Listening to people going about their daily business and the traffic trundling through the village did not have the same appeal.

To give Bruno his due, though, he had spent a lot of time down here sorting things out while she'd packed up their personal belongings and prepared the auberge for handing over to Libby. The mas had not been lived in since Bruno's mother died two years ago, and Odette had made him promise to clean it thoroughly before she moved in. But it still needed a lot doing to it.

'We can decorate and get it to our taste slowly,' she'd told him. 'But we need a proper bathroom and I want a new kitchen.' For years she'd dreamt about having a kitchen designed just for her. Whatever Bruno said, it had to be the first thing, together with a new salle de bain, to be done in their new home. Her reward for leaving the auberge and her life there.

He'd been as good as his word and in the eight weeks it took for all the legal paperwork to go through, a new kitchen and a new bathroom had been installed. If only she felt like using the new kitchen; but somehow cooking was the last thing she felt like doing these days.

Odette moved across to the boxes in the centre of the room. Better get on with it and at least try to make the place look a bit more like home.

An hour later she was putting the last of the books on the shelves when Bruno returned. 'Everything good at the au . . . Libby's?' She knew that was where he'd been. Something about collecting some tools he'd left in the garden shed, showing Libby the secret places where the hens sometimes laid their eggs. He'd suggested that Odette go with him and have a coffee with Libby but she'd declined. Initially she thought she'd spend a lot of time up at the auberge helping Libby settle in, but she'd realised it wasn't a good idea for her to hang around up there too much. She knew Libby would always ask if she needed help or advice.

'You've been busy up here,' Bruno said, looking at the empty boxes waiting to be thrown away, their contents now displayed around the room.

'I need to hang the curtains next. Maybe then it will start to feel cosy.'

Bruno sighed, hearing the downbeat tone to her voice, before putting his arm around her and drawing her close.

'*Chérie*, this has to be for the best. The Auberge was too much for you — us — now. Life changes and we have to accept that.'

'It is not such a big wrench for you,' Odette said quietly. 'I know you're looking forward to living in your boyhood home again. But aren't you a teeny bit sad about leaving the auberge — our home since the day we married?' Her new home had been such a change from the old farm she'd grown up on down near Redon. She'd loved the challenge of turning the house first into a family home and then later into the Auberge du Canal. Slowly over the years, feeding and looking after the auberge's guests had become her raison d'être, especially when Isabelle had left home. And now it had been taken away from her.

Bruno nodded. '*Mais oui*. It's hard for you to leave, I realise, *ma cherie*, but it was time we retired. Took things easier.'

'I know, but we lived there for over

forty years. All our memories are there. Already I miss it so much after just two days.' Odette wiped a tear away with the back of her hand. 'The only good thing is that it is Libby who buys. I am very happy about that. It will be good having her living here in France. But I can't help but be sad about leaving.'

'We bring the memories with us,' Bruno said. 'Then make more here together. Life will be better for us in the village, you'll see. Less work, more fun. We'll be able to travel a bit. See more of Isabelle. Enjoy the freedom, and the rest of our lives.'

At the mention of their daughter, Odette remembered Bruno's earlier suggestion of spending time down on the Riviera. 'Visit her in Antibes? I would enjoy that. Shall we go soon?' She hugged Bruno back. Maybe there would be some compensation for leaving her beloved auberge after all.

'*Bon*. It is agreed we go soon,' Bruno said.

Odette glanced at her watch. 'I'd

better go and start lunch.'

'I have an idea, *ma cherie*,' Bruno said. 'Why don't we have lunch in the village café? Less work and *peut-être* it will cheer you up.'

★ ★ ★

Two hours later and back from lunch, Odette thrust the fork into the weed-infested soil and leaned on the handle, catching her breath. Getting to grips with this overgrown jungle of a garden was proving harder than she'd anticipated.

Gardening at the auberge had consisted mainly of looking after geranium-filled pots, a couple of flower borders, and the occasional pruning of the back hedge. Bruno had grown their vegetables in a plot securely fenced off from the ducks and the chickens, while the rest of the grounds had been used for guest parking.

Here at the village mas she had both the land and the free time to indulge herself in what she was beginning to suspect could easily become an obsession. There was a lot of work to be done. Bruno had cut the lawn before they moved in but nothing else had been touched for years. Looking around her now, she could see primroses, daffodils and miniature cyclamen all at various stages of growth in the old flower beds. The rambling roses over the old arched pergola were already budding up. Closing her eyes, she imagined sitting out under its perfumed shade of a summer's afternoon, enjoying the tranquility.

The patch of ground she was currently clearing was the sunniest and warmest spot in the garden. A buddleia had spread its branches out along the back wall but there was plenty of space for more trees and shrubs when she'd decided what she wanted. She must admit to quite fancying an olive tree.

Bruno had promised he'd clean out the old pond and re-stock it with some fish. Maybe they'd even get some visiting frogs. Many a summer night Odette had gone to sleep listening to the croaking of the canal frogs.

Outside the kitchen door the old granite trough was filled with compost waiting for her to plant it up with the herbs she wanted. Basil, parsley, chives, sage and thyme were all on order down at the garden centre.

'Odette. Ready to go to the pepinère in five minutes?' As if reading her thoughts, Bruno's voice startled her out of her daydreaming. She'd forgotten the herbs were ready for collecting today.

'Better make it ten,' she said, hurrying indoors to wash her hands and change her shoes.

The garden centre was buzzing as they drove in. Spring-like weather over the past few days had infused people with the enthusiasm for sorting out their winter-ravaged gardens.

While Bruno went to pay for the herbs and put them in the car, Odette wandered down through the pepinère to where the large shrubs and trees were. She was standing looking at a willow tree when Bruno found her. 'D'you think we could plant a willow? It would look wonderful by the pond,' she said. 'It would be a real statement in that part of the garden. They're such elegant trees. I love the way everything moves in a gentle breeze, like it's dancing.'

'Let's go and find Pascal and see whether he thinks we have the right conditions.'

'He's here today?' Odette said, surprised. Only last week they'd attended the funeral of Gilles de Guesclin, Pascal's father and Bruno's friend from schooldays, and one of the biggest landowners in the area. As his only son, Pascal had inherited the estate which included a small chateau, a couple of farms and the garden centre, which had always been Pascal's responsibility. 'I'd have thought he'd be too busy sorting everything else out.'

Bruno nodded. 'You know how much he's always loved this place. I was saying just now how being down here with the plants helps him to think straight. It's his sanctuary from the world.'

'Where is he now? Still in the office?' Odette said.

Bruno nodded and they began to make their way up through an enormous poly-tunnel to the office area, where they found Pascal busy checking off a delivery of plants with an assistant.

'Odette.' Pascal kissed her cheek. 'How are you?'

'*Ca va*,' Odette said. 'You? How are you coping?' she asked gently. 'Your mother too?'

'She's not good but she copes. Now what can I do for you?'

When he heard what they were interested in buying, he left his assistant to finish with the delivery and walked down to help them decide which willow tree would be the best for their garden. When they'd settled on a well-established one at about eight feet tall, Odette said, 'I have a fancy for an olive tree too. I know it's a Mediterranean

66

tree, but there is a very sheltered part of the garden that gets lots of sun, and an olive tree would just be perfect there.'

'I'm sorry, Odette, but I don't have an olive tree in stock. I can get you one, though, and there is no reason why in the spot you describe it wouldn't prosper. You'd have to protect its roots in winter from frost, of course, but they can survive temperatures of minus seven degrees.'

'How long to wait for one?' Odette asked.

Pascal shrugged. 'Two, maybe three weeks. Leave the willow tree here and I deliver them both together, yes?'

'Perfect,' Odette said. 'Thank you.'

Leaving Pascal to return to work, Odette and Bruno made their way back to the car.

'Such a shame Pascal has never married,' Odette said. 'He should really have a wife and family by now. He has to think about his own inheritance too. Perhaps his father dying will finally encourage him to find someone. I would like to see him happy.'

'You're forgetting about his mother,' Bruno said. 'It will take someone special to cope with her. Someone who is strong enough to stand up for herself.'

Odette glanced at Bruno. Sometimes he still surprised her with his insight. 'Ah yes, I'd forgotten how she likes to control the lives of the men in her family. Poor Pascal will now be the sole receiver of her attention!'

4

Libby

On her way to the kitchen to make herself a coffee, Libby picked up the reservations book from the hall table. Ever since Odette had said the rally was marked in there, she'd been meaning to look and see if there were any other bookings she needed to know about.

May appeared to be a popular month. June, too, was busy, and there were several Saturday-night dinner tables already reserved throughout the year. Lots of bookings for July and August, several for September, and the vintage motor club was already pencilled in for its Christmas 'do'. Maybe they'd cancel if the rally tea this week didn't come up to their expectations. Which it would. Now she'd agreed to do it, Libby was determined it would be a success. If only to show the vet Lucas that she wasn't as ditzy as he'd clearly thought she was that day on the canal path.

In between the bookings Libby found little notes that Odette had left her. 'Boiler service this week'; 'Habitation tax due this week'; 'Chateauneuf market is the first and the third Wednesday every month'.

Heavily underlined on the first page of August was: 'Remember EVERY-ONE goes on holiday this month! It is impossible to get a plumber, electrician or carpenter — or a dentist!'

Libby realised Odette had left her a veritable handbook of how to run an auberge for the inexperienced. She had a feeling she was going to come to regard this reservation book as her 'how-to bible' over the coming months.

At the back of the book under 'Contacts' was a list of useful telephone numbers, including one for the French magazine advertising department that Odette used on a regular basis. Resolutely, Libby picked up the phone. She needed to keep the business coming in, so she'd stick with Odette's advertising while she worked out an advertising strategy of her own.

Half an hour later, when her French had been severely tested by the superior-sounding woman on the other end of the phone, Libby picked up the 'how-to bible' again. The entry for the 'Rally Tea' leapt out at her.

Remembering what Odette had said about the food required, Libby began to make a list of things she'd need to buy. She hadn't yet done a supermarket shop to stock her store-cupboard, so the usual basics would have to be bought too. Stocking the kitchen from scratch. She and Chloe would go later in the week. In the meantime she wanted to take a proper look at the gîte and decide what needed doing.

Converted years ago by Bruno and Odette from what had originally been a traditional stone agricultural building, the rustic charm of the interior was starting to look shabby. A thin layer of dust over everything didn't help either. Exposed stonework, ceiling beams, wooden floors and a wood-burning stove did give the place a certain ambience, however.

Glancing into the small salle de bain, Libby wondered how she could update it all without spending a fortune. If it wasn't going to earn its keep she didn't want to throw money at it this year. Maybe just a good clean and rearrange the furniture.

She was standing there mentally rearranging the furniture when the gîte door opened and Chloe walked in. 'Mum, can I talk to you?'

Libby glanced at her. 'What's wrong?'

'Nothing. It's just that . . . ' Chloe fiddled with her hair, a sure sign she was nervous. 'Before we came out here I heard about a part-time job that would be absolutely perfect for me — and the day before we left I had an interview.'

Libby's heart sank. 'You've got it? You're leaving?'

'I haven't heard yet, but it means I'd

be leaving you on your own earlier than planned if I do get it. Which is unlikely anyway, as so many people will be after it. I just thought I'd better warn you.'

'What's the job anyway?'

'Intern on a London magazine. The experience would look good on my CV when I finish college.'

'You're right, a lot of people will be after that,' Libby said. 'Where were you planning on living if you get the job? Your student accommodation won't be available until the new term.'

'I was hoping that Auntie Helen would give me bed and board.' Chloe glanced at her mother. 'I feel so guilty even thinking about leaving you.'

Libby held up her hand. 'Stop it, Chloe. You have no reason to feel guilty about anything. This is my new life, not yours. Yours is college, hopefully followed by a career in journalism. Of course I want you here with me for as long as possible, but we always knew you were going back to the UK in September.' Which she'd secretly been dreading anyway, but she wasn't about to tell Chloe that.

Chloe hugged her. 'Thanks, Mum. Fancy a cuppa? I'll go and put the kettle on.'

'I'll just lock up here,' Libby said as Chloe left. Despite her insisting to Chloe that this attempt to make a new life in France was hers and hers alone, she'd been looking forward to sharing the first few months with Chloe. Still, there was no guarantee that Chloe would get the job — hundreds of would-be journalists must have applied — in which case she'd stay here.

Guiltily Libby pushed the wish away that Chloe wouldn't get the internship for the purely selfish reason that she didn't feel ready to cope with the auberge without having her daughter around.

★ ★ ★

On the morning of the rally Libby was up early. With Napoleon the cockerel shouting out his wake-up calls any time from 4.30 onwards, she didn't need an alarm clock, that was for sure.

She'd quickly developed an early-morning routine: Shower, dress, cup of tea, and then out to feed the chickens and ducks, before heading back into the kitchen to make breakfast for herself and Chloe.

Libby loved spending early-morning time alongside what she already thought of as her stretch of canal. Some mornings there was a mist hovering over everything; other mornings the sun had already broken through with the promise of a beautiful day. This morning there was a heron high up in one of the trees on the opposite bank. She'd stood watching as he took off, unhurriedly making his way along the canal.

Back indoors she put the three eggs she'd found in the hen house on the table and called out to Chloe. 'Fancy scrambled eggs for breakfast?'

'Mmm, sounds great. Down in five.'

Two days ago she and Chloe had

done a big supermarket shop, stocking up on basic kitchen ingredients and the food for the rally. This morning she planned on making quiches, soup, a couple of sponges and some biscuits for the rally tea in the afternoon. Odette was joining them later to help with the cooking and was also bringing the bread for the sandwiches from the boulangerie and some ham for the baguettes from the village butcher.

Over breakfast she and Chloe made lists and planned the morning's baking. By the time Odette arrived mid-morning the kitchen was a hub of activity: sponges cooling on the rack, soup bubbling on the stove, quiches cooking, and full biscuit tins.

Libby looked at Odette anxiously. 'Is all this OK? What the men — I presume it's mainly men — will be expecting?'

Odette nodded. 'It's fine. They are always hungry when they return.' She put the crash-hat she was carrying down on the table by the door. 'I have told Bruno I will go with him this afternoon if we get everything ready before they leave, and you can manage without me.'

'You ride pillion?' Chloe said. 'Aren't you — '

'*Oui*. It's how we meet a long time ago.' She looked at Chloe. 'I'm sure you weren't going to say I'm too old, were you, Chloe?' Odette said, looking at her.

'No, of course not. I was going to ask, aren't you frightened on the back?' Chloe said. 'It's just that motorbikes terrify me. I can't imagine ever wanting to ride one.'

'Oh but Chloe, they are such fun. Maybe one day you go with Bruno and . . . '

'No,' Chloe interrupted vehemently, causing both Libby and Odette to look at her in surprise. 'Sorry. But no thank you. I'll make a start on the sand-wiches.'

Odette shrugged before turning to Libby. 'Bruno has always had motor-cycles, but it is a long time since I've been able to go on the opening club outing with him. But only if we have everything organised. I'll be back to help you serve anyway.'

'We'll make sure we are organised,' Libby said.

It was two o'clock when the club members began to arrive. Cars and motorcycles jostled for space in the parking area and on the canal path. One of the first to arrive was Pascal, and Odette quickly introduced him to Libby.

'Unfortunately I can't ride this afternoon. I have to get back to the garden centre, but as president of the club I like to send them on their way,' he said, smiling at Libby as he shook her hand. 'I return for tea. Please keep me a slice of that delicious-looking gâteau. The chocolate one.'

Lucas was one of the last to arrive and Libby gazed in admiration at his car as he parked. As Odette had said, it was a beautiful vintage Delage which, with its gleaming cream and dark-blue bodywork and classic sports-car shape, looked as though it was starring centre stage on a 1930s film set.

'*Bonjour*,' he said, striding over to Libby, where Odette made the official introductions.

'I know you've met in passing. But Libby, this is Lucas, our local vet and owner of the most lusted-after car in the area,' Odette said. 'Lucas — Libby.'

'Nice to meet you, Libby. Thank you for not cancelling this afternoon.' Her hand, taken in a firm grasp, was left tingling when he let go and turned to Pascal. 'How are things? You joining us today for once?'

Pascal shook his head. '*Non*. Duty calls until six o'clock, when I'll be back. Enjoy the drive. Don't get lost today.'

'Do people often get lost on these rallies?' Libby asked.

Lucas shook his head. 'Only when Pascal here does the map directions. Today Bruno has done them so it will all be good, eh, Odette?'

Odette nodded. '*Je pense* it's time to

get going,' she said.

Libby and Chloe joined Pascal as he stood watching the cavalcade depart. Lucas, the last to leave, gave them a wave and a toot on his horn as he followed Bruno and Odette out onto the path. As he too disappeared, Pascal jumped on his motorbike. 'Must get back to the pepinère. I return for the gateau later!'

'Lots of sexy Frenchmen around here,' Chloe said, glancing her Libby. 'You'll be spoilt for choice!'

'Chloe, stop it!' Libby laughed. 'The last thing I need right now is a man in my life. Come on, let's get organised for their return.' There was definitely no room in it for a sexy Frenchman. She'd got far too much to do for the foreseeable future, sorting out the auberge.

For the next couple of hours Libby and Chloe were busy setting out crockery, cutlery and glasses as well as the food on the long trestle table they'd set up on the lawn at the side of the auberge. At least the sun was shining, so they could eat outdoors.

Noticing the mobile phone sticking out of the back pocket of Chloe's jeans, Libby said, 'Not heard yet then?'

Chloe shook her head. 'Doesn't look as if I got it. Today was the date of notification.'

'Doesn't necessarily mean they've kept to it,' Libby said, placing the first of three large quiches on the table. 'Sometimes things get delayed.' Looking at the despondent droop to Chloe's shoulders, though, she knew her daughter didn't believe her. 'And don't forget the time difference.'

With ten minutes to go before they could expect the first drivers to arrive back for the celebration tea, they'd finished setting everything out. Libby, looking at the table with its bright yellow-and-blue tablecloth laden with all the food she'd prepared, breathed a sigh of relief. It looked good, but the real test would come when people started to eat.

Bruno and Odette were among the

first riders to return and Odette immediately joined Libby to help serve the food, which seemed to be disappearing at an alarming rate.

'Don't worry, they'll slow down in a moment,' Odette whispered.

'Is everybody here?' Libby asked, frantically trying to count heads. Had more than the 30 people she'd been told to expect turned up? 'Have I made enough food?'

'Lucas isn't back yet. A couple of bikers have probably gone straight home, and Pascal we know will be late,' Odette said. 'So, yes I think we have enough. It's delicious, too, so stop worrying.'

Libby cut a generous slice of chocolate cake and put it to one side. 'Pascal,' she said, 'asked me to save him a piece.' She glanced across at Chloe down at the other end of the table talking animatedly into her mobile phone. Her heart sank.

Chloe flashed her a quick smile and gave her a thumbs up sign. Did that mean she'd got the job?

'Ah, here's Lucas,' Odette said as the mud-splattered vintage car drew to a stop.

As Lucas stepped out of the car and made his way over to Libby and the food, Chloe switched off her phone, looked at Libby and mouthed, 'I've got it!'

'Your daughter looks happy,' Lucas said.

'Mmm,' Libby said absently. 'I think she's just got a job — back in England.' She sighed.

'Is that a problem for you?' Lucas asked, taking the plate of food she handed him.

'I'm pleased for her but I shall miss her terribly. I'd hoped she'd be here for the summer. The main problem, though, is I shall now have to find another car quickly.' She'd promised Chloe her car when she returned to the UK, knowing she needed to buy a left-hand drive one once she was settled in. 'I thought I'd have more time to find one.'

'You know about cars?' Lucas asked.

'No. Dan, my husband, always used to deal with things like that. I'm a total dunce when it comes to all things mechanical.'

Lots of things had been a steep learning curve when Dan died — finances, insurance, surviving — but Libby knew she'd never master the art of telling a good car from a bad car. She'd have to trust the garage on that.

'Me, I know a lot about cars,' Lucas said. 'If you like, I can help you find one.'

Libby looked at him, surprised. 'Thank you, if you're not too busy. I have to warn you, though, I can't afford vintage!'

'I will ask around. I also have a friend with a garage in Quimper. He will help as well if necessary.'

As Libby went to say thank you again, a taxi pulled up on the canal path and she watched as the driver got out and looked around before making his way over to Odette.

'You have guests arriving today?' Lucas asked.

Libby shook her head. 'No. My first guests aren't due until next weekend.' She waited as Odette and the taxi driver made their way over to her.

'Andre has a passenger who would like to stay. He forget when he bring her here that I'm not the owner now. But I tell him that's not a problem,' Odette said. 'His passenger is welcome.'

'But I'm not open,' Libby protested. 'Isn't there anywhere else locally the taxi driver can take her? I'm really not ready.'

Odette wagged a finger at her. 'Libby, you 'ave a business now. You 'ave to take the guests when they come. Andre here always recommends me with the tourists. You turn him away today, perhaps he no come with others. You have a room ready, *oui?*'

Libby nodded slowly. She had this feeling that once again she was being bulldozed by Odette into agreeing to accept her first guest.

'The lady has been ill and she wants simply to rest and recover in the countryside for a week.'

Libby took a deep breath. 'Ok. I'll just go and check the room while Andre gets her things out of the taxi.'

No time now to put a vase of fresh flowers on the dressing table, but Libby grabbed a box of Bretagne biscuits from the kitchen to put on the tea tray she'd set up on all the bedside tables.

Libby had a quick look around the front bedroom to satisfy herself that everything was in order and there were enough towels and soaps in the en-suite bathroom before going back down-stairs, ready to greet her first guest.

Her first thought when she saw the woman standing in the hallway was how frail she appeared. 'She's so thin,' Libby whispered to Chloe. 'She must have been very ill.'

Moving across to the woman, Libby said, 'Welcome to the Auberge du Canal, Madam . . . ?'

'Patem. Madame Evie Patem.'

Libby smiled. 'If you will follow me, Madame Patem, I will show you to your room.'

Slowly Madam Patem followed Libby up the stairs, leaning heavily on the bannister for support at one point. Libby glanced at her, concerned. Was her first guest going to be a liability?

'If you need anything please ask,' Libby said, opening the bedroom door. 'Breakfast is at eight-thirty — if that time's all right for you?'

'I never eat breakfast, so it is not important. Just coffee please. Now I sleep — it's been a long day. Thank you. I will see you in the morning.' And the bedroom door was firmly closed behind Madame Patem.

Feeling as though she'd been dismissed, Libby made her way back downstairs and out to the remnants of the rally tea. Odette glanced at her.

'Everything all right with Madame Patem?'

Libby nodded. 'Think so. She doesn't look well though. Hope she doesn't collapse on me.'

★　★　★

The next morning, Libby poured a mug of coffee and pushed it across the kitchen table to Chloe. 'Can't believe you're really going today. So quickly.'

Chloe nodded. 'It'll give me a couple of days to settle in at Aunt Helen's and psyche myself up for work.' She hesitated before continuing. 'Are you sure you're all right about me leaving you here alone?'

'Of course. Besides, I'm not alone.' Libby jerked her head up towards the ceiling. 'I have a guest. And more booked in for next week.'

'I still feel guilty though,' Chloe said quietly. 'I know we'd planned . . . '

'Chloe, stop it. This internship's a great opportunity for you. Make sure you make the most of it. Anyway, you'll be back for a holiday before you start college, won't you?'

'Probably even before — just for a weekend,' Chloe said. 'Depending on how much work they give me.'

'Good. Now about the car. It had a full service before we came over so there shouldn't be any problems, but don't forget to check the tyre pressures before you leave. I'm sure Uncle Pete will keep an eye on it for you over there.'

'Mum! Stop fussing. That's another thing. How will you manage until you buy a car?' Chloe looked at her mother worriedly.

'I can walk into the village — I can find most things there. Anyway, Lucas has promised to help me find a car quickly — and more importantly, he'll check it over before I buy,' Libby said.

Chloe looked at her but before she could say anything the phone rang.

Libby got up to answer it. 'Good morning, Odette.'

There was silence in the kitchen as Libby listened before saying, 'Thank you. Yes, I'll tell her.'

Replacing the receiver, Libby said, 'Odette thinks I'm going to be upset and lonely when you've gone, so she's invited me to lunch one day next week. Think she wants to show off her new kitchen. She wishes you all the best for your job, by the way. She's going to try and pop up later to say goodbye.'

'Right. I'm going to finish packing and then load the car.' Chloe stood up.

'When you're ready I'll help you carry stuff down,' Libby said. 'Oh, *bonjour*, Madame Patem. Can I get you a coffee?'

'Please,' Evie said.

Libby, about to suggest that Evie go into the dining room, decided against it and pointed to the chair Chloe had just left. One of the things she'd always liked about staying with Odette was the friendly 'make yourself at home' atmosphere that things like taking coffee in the kitchen generated. She was determined to continue the tradition.

Libby placed a mug of coffee in front of Evie. Evie looked as if she could do with some company this morning.

'Milk? Sugar? Toast?'

Evie shook her head. 'Just black coffee. Is there a pharmacy in the village? I think perhaps I ought to have this checked. I had a fall a couple of days ago.' She pulled the sleeve of her jumper up so Libby could see the bruising and swelling around her elbow.

'Nasty. I'm sure the pharmacy will check it out for you. I'll ring for a taxi, shall I? Unless you want to walk in with me later?'

Evie shook her head. 'In my fall I also hurt my ankle. I can't walk too far. A taxi will be fine.'

'I'd offer to take you,' Libby said, 'but Chloe is taking the car today.' She quickly explained about Chloe's job.

'You will miss her,' Evie said.

Libby nodded. 'Of course. But children have to fly the nest, don't they? D'you have any?'

Evie shook her head. 'No.' She took a sip of her coffee.

Libby broke the silence that followed Evie's brief answer. 'I know you said you don't eat breakfast, but what about lunch? Dinner?'

Evie shrugged. 'I'll pick something up in the village. I don't eat a lot anyway. I've got some energy bars upstairs.'

Libby hesitated before saying, 'Why don't you have a kitchen supper with me this evening? On the house. It would be nice to have company this evening,' she added quietly. 'Chloe will have gone by then.'

There was a slight pause before Evie said, '*D'accord*. I look forward to it. Now, perhaps you could help me organise a taxi?'

5

Odette and Libby

When Pascal rang to say he'd received the olive tree earlier than expected and could he bring it and the willow tree over, Odette agreed immediately. 'Thanks, and Pascal, could you bring a couple of bags of compost with you please?'

Between them she and Bruno dug a hole by the pond for the willow and a smaller one at the far end of the garden for the olive tree. Now, as she waited for Pascal to arrive, Odette wandered around the garden visualising how it would look in a few months' time when all her new plants and shrubs were settled in.

She was pleased to see that the old wisteria plant over the loggia was already leafy and in bud. With the teak table and chairs placed underneath, it would be a perfect spot for lunch with

Libby later in the week.

When Pascal arrived Bruno left the kitchen garden which he'd been digging over and gave him a hand carrying the trees into the garden. 'D'you want a hand planting them?' Pascal asked.

Bruno shook his head. 'No, it's fine. We manage between us.'

'Pascal, come to lunch on Thursday,' Odette said impulsively as she walked back to his truck with him. 'I'm planning a mini-celebration now we're more or less settled here.'

As Pascal hesitated she continued, 'I know your mama goes to the card club in the village for lunch then, so you don't have to worry about her, and you close between twelve and three o'clock. Do come.' Knowing how notoriously shy Pascal was, she added, 'It's only us and Libby.'

Pascal smiled his thanks. 'Quarter past twelve OK? I look forward to it.'

'Good. Now I'll go give Bruno a hand,' Odette said.

The olive tree was quickly planted in

its new home in the sunniest corner of the garden. The larger willow took some time and persuasion to stand upright by the pond, but finally it was firmly placed in the ground and secured to a tall stake.

'Right,' Odette said. 'I'm going to walk up to the auberge and see Libby. She'll be missing Chloe today I think. Are you coming?'

Bruno shook his head. 'While you're gone I want to make a start on clearing the pond.'

'I do love you,' Odette said, leaning forward to kiss his cheek in a rare display of emotion. 'I will cook you a special meal tonight.'

'Chicken in your wine sauce? Raspberry pavlova?'

'I'll be back in an hour to organise it,' Odette promised, picking up her bag and coat.

Making her way through the village, Odette turned left and took the long flight of narrow steps down the side of *La Poste* and stepped onto the canal path. Five minutes later she was opening the auberge gate. The door of the gîte was open and Odette could see Libby inside rearranging furniture.

'Hi,' Libby said, panting from the exertion of pushing the two-seater settee into its new position under the window. 'Just giving the place a bit of an airing and thought I'd change things around a bit. What d'you think?'

Odette nodded. 'Looks better. You have bookings for it?'

'No,' Libby said. 'I wanted to get it ready for the summer.' She glanced across at Odette. 'Did you use it much? I can't remember anybody staying in it any of the times we visited.'

'People seemed to prefer the auberge itself,' Odette said. 'I did rent it out for winter a few years ago, but there are so many gîtes around people are spoilt for choice.'

'I'll keep it for visiting family and friends then,' Libby said. 'Maybe at the end of the season see if anyone would like to rent it for winter.'

'Chloe get off all right?' Odette asked.

Libby smiled. 'Yes, and arrived safely. She sent me a text at midnight last night to tell me.'

'She woke you up?'

'No. Evie and I were still in the kitchen talking. I'd invited her to join me for supper,' Libby explained. 'Seemed silly not to when we were both alone.'

Last evening had turned into an unexpected girly evening as the two of them had got to know each other. 'Shame she's only here for a week before she returns to Paris,' Odette said.

'I think she's a very private person though. She didn't really tell me a lot about herself.'

Evie, who had assumed Libby was divorced, had been mortified when Libby had told her she was a widow. 'You are so brave starting a new life here, in a foreign country, alone. I do not think I could ever do that.'

Libby had shrugged. 'It's an adventure. If it doesn't work out I can always return to England. What do you do when you're not ill?' She remembered registering Evie's hesitant pause before she answered.

'I work in entertainment for the moment. I too am coming to — how you say — a crossroads in my life. I have to decide what to do next.'

'Where do you live?'

'Paris.'

'Well there'll be lots of opportunities up there for you I expect,' Libby had said.

Evie had shaken her head. 'I'm not so sure,' she said before changing the subject and asking Libby about Chloe and her planned career.

The rest of the evening had passed pleasantly, as they'd made each other giggle with stories about their different life experiences. Although Libby realised later that it was her life with Dan that had been the main subject of conversation. Not once had Evie mentioned having a partner or a boyfriend in her life.

Chloe's text message to reassure her

mother about her safe arrival at Helen's had been the signal for them to finally say good night and go to bed.

'You have made a new friend,' Odette said.

'You know, I think I have,' Libby said. 'Odette, can I talk to you about the guests who arrive next weekend? They're regulars, aren't they? Any tips on what they like and don't like? They want dinner every evening.'

Odette laughed. 'That would be the Bichets. They usually come at this time of year. You will like them. For dinner they like lots of salads and charcuterie, but they do not like garlic. They love chocolate desserts and they like their coffee really, really strong.'

'A non-garlic-liking French family? I don't believe it,' Libby laughed and turned as there was a gentle knock on the door.

'Hi. May I come in?' Evie said.

'*Bonjour*, Madame Patem,' Odette said politely.

'*Bonjour*,' Evie answered.

'How's your arm?' Libby asked.

'Still painful but better. The pharmacy gave me some ointment to help bring the bruising out. Suggested a sling, but . . . ' Evie shrugged. 'I prefer not. My ankle being strapped is enough. This is nice. You have guests coming in here?'

Libby shook her head. 'No. I'm going to keep it for when family and friends visit and the auberge is full. Chloe has a bedroom in my apartment so I'm not expecting this gîte to be used that much.' She looked at the expensive camera Evie had hanging around her neck. 'You're obviously a keen photographer — I wouldn't know where to start with a camera that complicated. Has to be a simple point and click for me!'

Evie smiled. 'It's easy really. I'm going to sit on the bench alongside the canal to take some photos. I saw a beautiful heron earlier. I would love to capture a picture of him.'

'Before you go, Madame Patem,

Libby is coming for lunch with Bruno and me on Thursday. Perhaps you would care to join us?' Odette smiled at Evie.

'That is very kind of you. I'd love to. And please, call me Evie. Thank you. Libby, I'll see you later.' Evie turned to make her way slowly towards the canal path.

6

Suzette / Evie

The next morning Napoleon, crowing just yards away from her bedroom window, startled Suzette into fitful consciousness. Not since her childhood had she been woken by such a raucous sound. Every morning since she'd arrived at the auberge it had taken her several seconds to realise what the noise was and where she actually was.

As realisation dawned, the same jumbled, panic-stricken thoughts began to stampede through her mind. What was she doing here? She'd been stupid to leave Monaco without telling someone — Malik, anyone — what she was planning to do. If anything happened to her here nobody would know.

Malik. How had he reacted when the hotel concierge had handed him her note? The press would know all about the accident by now. She could just see the headlines in the Nice *Matin*. 'Has a jeté too many finished accident-prone Suzette Shelby's career?'

As for telling Libby that she was Madame Evie Patem, what had she been thinking? Why was she trying to keep her whereabouts secret?

Did it really matter to the media where she recovered after this latest accident? Of course not. But she was so tired of fending off questions about injuries and about her imminent retirement. All they seemed to want to do was tell the world that she was past it.

Well she wasn't past it yet! With a week or two of country living and no stress in her life, her ankle would mend and she'd be ready to return to Paris and prepare for the autumn show.

Idly she reached out and picked up her mobile phone from the bedside table. Time to check for messages. The first text was from Malik: '*Cherie*, I hope you had a good journey back to

Paris. Look after yourself. I will see you next week when I return. L. xxx.' Below this there was now a whole new bunch of texts, all demanding to know where the hell she was.

He was clearly back in Paris and knew she'd gone awol. She felt a guilty pang now for switching off her mobile phone for the past few days to postpone the inevitable for as long as possible. She'd have to speak to him and try to explain; get him to understand her reasons.

Suzette's finger hovered over the reply button before she closed the phone and replaced it back on the table. Right now she couldn't face talking to him. Besides, Malik wasn't known for being an early riser. If she woke him he was sure to be grumpy with her. She'd leave it until later in the day.

Fully awake now, Suzette pushed the duvet away and got up, wincing as her right foot touched the floor. Her ankle, still swollen and painful as she took the support bandaging off, now sported a mass of psychedelic blue, black and yellow colours.

Ten minutes later Suzette collapsed back on the bed, exhausted from trying to stand and wash in the shower. It would have been easier to jump in the bath. Towelling her hair dry, she looked at the brown pixie-cut wig on the dressing table.

She'd been determined to keep her flight from Monaco out of the papers, and hiding her blonde hair under a wig with a totally different style to her normal hair had been the answer to her passing incognito through the airport. The question now was, did she continue to wear the wig and keep up the pretence here in the wilds of north-west France?

If she pushed Suzette Shelby into the background of her life for a week or two, would it help her to decide about life without dancing, or not? Was this the chance she needed to truly be herself? Decide which way to go for the rest of her life?

Apart from anything else, how embarrassing it would be to go downstairs and say, 'Actually Libby, my name is Suzette Shelby. I'm a ballerina. You may have heard of me.' The evening she'd had supper with Libby in the kitchen she'd felt so comfortable; felt that they were on similar wavelengths as well as age. The close confines of the world of dance she'd lived in for all her adult life until now meant that opportunities to make friends — proper girl friends — had passed her by. As Evie surely she would find it easier to make and keep Libby's friendship?

Decision made, she pulled the wig into position over her head. While she was staying at the Auberge du Canal she would be Evie, and leave the missing Suzette Shelby to deal with the world she'd left behind at a later date.

Her mobile buzzed. Malik. He was up early for once. Taking a deep breath, she pressed his number.

'Where the hell are you?' Malik demanded angrily when she answered.

'I've been out of my head with worry since I got back and discovered you'd disappeared. And why haven't you been answering my calls?'

Suzette sighed. She'd been dreading this conversation.

'I'm just having a holiday where no one knows who I am,' she said. 'I'm sorry you've been worried, but I'm fine.'

'You being fine isn't enough. For goodness sake, Suzette, the press will have a field day with you when they find out you've gone missing.'

'They don't have to find out,' Suzette said. 'I'm not planning on telling them, and I hope you won't. All I'm asking for is some private time to really think about my future.'

'Why can't you do that here in Paris?'

'Because I can't.' How to explain that everything crowded in on her there? It stopped her thinking coherently. Too many memories, too many might-have-beens, and definitely too many regrets about her life there. Here she was beginning to be able to truly step back and think about things dispassionately.

Malik was silent. Even down the phone line Suzette could sense his frustration.

'How did Monaco go in the end? Donna perform well?' she asked, hoping to change the conversation.

'Yes,' Malik said. 'She's a star in the making, that's for sure.'

It was Suzette's turn to be silent. So many years since that had been said about her.

'How's the ankle?' Malik asked.

'Responding well to gentle exercise,' Suzette said, guiltily standing on one leg and making a circling movement with the offending ankle. She'd totally forgotten about exercising it this weekend.

'Good. I presume you're still planning on doing *Swan Lake* with me? You'll need to be in tip-top condition for that.'

'No worries,' Suzette answered.

'So, exactly how long are you planning to stay wherever it is you are? Likely to be back before I go off to Geneva next weekend? Somebody there is interested in sponsoring a modern ballet I'm keen to choreograph so I have to go for a meet-up.'

'I think I'm going to stay a bit longer,' Suzette said. 'I'll talk to you when you get back.'

Although clearly disgruntled with that answer, Malik didn't press her on the subject again and the call ended.

Thoughtfully Suzette crossed over to the bedroom window and stared out at the canal and the woods on the far side. Down below in the auberge grounds, Napoleon and the chickens were enjoying dust baths over by the fence.

She'd not been entirely truthful with Malik when she'd told him she intended to stay a bit longer. If she was brave enough to put the idea that had occurred to her in the middle of the night into practice, she would be here for the whole of the summer. Alone and anonymous, with nobody from her real world having any idea where she was.

She just hoped she could persuade

Libby about the feasibility of her idea. She'd wait a couple of days before putting the suggestion to her. Crossing her fingers tightly, Evie hoped Libby wouldn't dismiss the idea out of hand.

7

Odette

Odette hummed softly to herself as she weighed, chopped and mixed various ingredients for the recipes she was preparing for the Thursday celebratory lunch she was cooking. Not yet nine o'clock, though she'd been busy for a couple of hours and already the results of her labours were showing.

Looking around her new kitchen, Odette sighed with satisfaction. The yeasty bread rolls were rising nicely in the small oven of her new top-of-the-range cooker, the duck was marinading in a red wine sauce on the worktop, and the roulade filled with chocolate cream and covered with white chocolate was rolled up and in the fridge.

Her wonderful modern kitchen was living up to all her expectations; she was going to be so happy preparing meals in here. She'd forgotten how much she enjoyed feeding friends and family. When Isabelle had left home, guests at the auberge had filled the cooking gap in her life, but now there was only Bruno to feed regularly. She'd have to invite friends around more often, she decided.

The sun was shining in through the kitchen window and she could see the willow tree with its newly green leafy fronds quivering in the gentle breeze as she set the coffee to brew. Bruno came in just as the coffee finished percolating.

'Good timing,' she said, reaching for two cups. 'Biscuit?'

'Thanks. Furniture cleaned and back out under the loggia ready for lunch,' Bruno said. 'We could sit out there now.'

Sitting companionably drinking their coffee, Odette said, 'Everything's beginning to come together here. I'm really looking forward to today's lunch, although I hope I've done the right thing inviting Evie.'

Bruno glanced at her, surprised. 'Why?'

'I told Pascal it would be just Libby. You know how shy he can be with strangers and I don't think he'd have agreed to come if he thought it would be more than just the three of us. I didn't think about him when I invited Evie.'

Bruno shrugged. 'It's not as if it's a huge crowd. Pascal will be fine. It's only when his mother is around that he tends to clam up. You haven't invited her, have you?'

Odette laughed. '*Non.*' She hesitated before adding, 'I hope Libby and Pascal get on.'

Bruno wagged a finger at her. 'You're not matchmaking, are you?'

Odette shook her head. '*Non.* But they are both single, so . . . '

'So you plan to help them along,' Bruno said, smiling. 'Lunch should be interesting.'

Libby and Evie arrived together promptly at twelve o'clock in the village taxi. Evie, knowing there was still no way her ankle was up to walking to Odette and Bruno's, had invited Libby to share the ride.

They were both sipping an aperitif with Odette and Bruno when Pascal arrived. Odette quickly introduced Evie to Pascal.

'*Enchanté*, mademoiselle,' he said, shaking her hand. 'I hope you enjoy your stay in Brittany.' He looked at her for several seconds before adding, 'Would we have met before?'

Evie laughed. 'I don't think so. I only arrived a few days ago.'

'Evie lives in Paris,' Libby said. 'So unless you frequent the city?'

Pascal visibly blanched at her words. 'I hate cities so rarely go. Even to Paris.' He turned again to Evie. 'It must be that you remind me of someone else.'

Once their starters were finished — individual walnut and onion tarts with a salad — Odette placed the duck with asparagus and sautéd potatoes on the table to accompanying cries of delight. 'Enjoy.'

'This is so delicious,' Libby said a few

minutes later. 'I have a favour to ask,' she said, addressing Odette. 'I'm going to need some help during the daytime and with the evening meals, especially at weekends. Any chance of you being free? Just until I've got into the swing of things. Only if you've got time and want to,' she added. 'If not, can you recommend someone?'

Odette sighed. 'Libby, I'd love to.' She glanced at Bruno. 'But Bruno here, he no want me to work every day.'

Bruno shrugged his shoulders. 'You decide, but remember our plan to have several *vacances* this year.'

'Maybe I come just on Saturdays?' Odette said. 'I will tell a woman in the village, Agnes, that you need help. She is a good worker.'

'Thanks,' Libby said. Hopefully this Agnes would be as good as Odette said.

Odette offered the wine to everyone before saying, 'I'm thinking about starting a monthly ladies' supper club here. I miss the cooking, and now I have this wonderful new kitchen I must put it to use. I feed Bruno too much he will get fat.'

'Brilliant idea,' Libby said. 'Can I be your first member?'

'It is a shame to limit it to the ladies though,' Pascal said. 'Why not a supper club open to all?'

'Maybe that would be a better idea,' Odette said.

It was two hours later, after the roulade had been eaten and the coffee and petit fours served, when Pascal pushed his chair back and apologised. 'Odette, that was a wonderful lunch but I am sorry, I have to go back to work.' He turned to Libby and Evie. 'May I offer you both a lift back to the auberge?'

'I need to do some things in the village before I go home,' Libby said. 'But I'm sure Evie would appreciate a lift.'

Evie nodded. 'Thank you. I was going to call the taxi.' The telephone rang as they were all saying their goodbyes and Bruno went to answer it.

Odette was alone and clearing the

table when he came back outside. 'Who was it?' she asked absently, piling plates on top of each other.

'Isabelle.'

Odette looked at him sharply. 'Is something the matter? It is not like Isabelle to ring during the day.'

'She is coming up for a weekend next month,' Bruno said.

Odette smiled. 'What a treat. How long is she staying?'

'She didn't say.'

'Is Laurent coming with her?'

Bruno shook his head. 'No. She is coming on her own.'

'I expect he's too busy at work to take the time,' Odette said before seeing the look on Bruno's face.

'She said she wants to talk to us about the future.' Bruno paused. 'I think Isabelle is maybe planning on coming back to Brittany permanently. But I'm not so sure Laurent is in agreement.'

Odette looked at him in dismay. Surely not. She couldn't bear it if Isabelle's marriage had failed.

8

Libby

Life, Libby found, was slipping into a routine. One that she realised was bound to get busier as the season wore on and the auberge filled with visitors. Mornings she was up early to feed the chickens and ducks before letting them out; egg collecting came later in the day. A quick croissant and coffee before starting on breakfasts for the guests and making her to-do list for the day.

Odette had warned her that while running the auberge would be fun and interesting, it would also be harder as single woman, but she hadn't realised just how hard it would turn out to be.

Thankfully Agnes, the woman whom Odette had recommended, had agreed to come in for two hours every day, starting next month when the auberge would be full for several weeks. Hopefully by then she'd be feeling more confident about coping with her new life.

She'd thought she was getting used to life without Dan, but since arriving in France all her despairing emotions of two years ago had surprised her by resurfacing. Shaking them off was proving even harder this time. She kept telling herself, *Buying the auberge was my decision, nobody else's*. Deep down she was convinced it had been a good choice; she just hadn't prepared herself mentally to face the many memories being alone in a place they'd both loved that were being stirred up daily.

Dan's presence seemed to be everywhere. Out on the terrace drinking a glass of rosé with her. Striding alongside her on the canal path as she walked into the village. Watching her in the kitchen while she prepared food. Every time she took his old toolbox out of the shed to do some little repair job she half expected him to take it out of her hands saying, 'This is a job for me.'

He'd always been a bit chauvinistic over DIY. She'd been happy to let him do things his way but now she was learning how to do stuff herself. Nothing major — refreshing the grouting in the bathroom and screwing the latch securely onto the chicken-house door had been her limit so far.

What she really missed was his companionship. At the end of the day, sitting out on her balcony with a glass of wine, she longed to be able to talk to him — go over the day's events; laugh at some incident together.

And yet, when Helen rang to say she was booking a ferry ticket and would be over in a couple of weeks, Libby had hesitated before agreeing. Not sure she was ready for the family memories having her sister-in-law around would drag up, she'd initially tried to put her off. But Helen had been surprisingly determined to come, muttering something about needing to get away for a bit.

Now, as the date for Helen's arrival

drew closer, Libby realised how much she was looking forward to having Helen staying at the auberge.

★ ★ ★

Two days after lunch at Odette's, Libby was tidying the kitchen and planning to spend the afternoon getting to grips with the weeds in the front garden when Lucas rang.

'Hi. Are you free this afternoon? I've heard about a car that might suit you. The problem is it's down in Morbihan, so it'll take a couple of hours to get there and back. You have dinner guests this evening?'

'No — only Evie, and she's not bothered what time she eats, if she eats at all. But can you afford the time to take me?'

'I have a few hours off until evening surgery. I'll pick you up in fifteen minutes.'

Libby sighed as she replaced the receiver. That was the gardening put off yet again then. She'd been expecting to not exactly have time on her hands when she moved to France, but certainly to live a more leisurely pace of life, giving her time to do things. Instead it had been non-stop almost from the time she'd put the key in the auberge door — and that was before any proper guests arrived expecting breakfast and dinner.

She ran upstairs to freshen up, slap some makeup on and get her bag. No need to change. That was another thing about living here. In the summer unexpected guests could arrive any time, so Libby was trying to get into the habit of being what her mother would have called 'presentable' at all times. Whether she would have viewed the jeans and T-shirt Libby generally wore these days as being 'presentable', Libby didn't dare think about. She pulled a pink sweatshirt over the T-shirt and combed her hair before applying a dab of lipstick.

She pushed a small sigh of disappointment away when Lucas arrived in his muddy estate car. A drive in the vintage Delage would have been nice. A poignant smell assaulted her nose as she opened the car door — a mixture of disinfectant and antiseptic.

Lucas smiled as he registered her involuntary gasp.

'Smells like a hospital in here,' she said.

'*Desolé*. It comes with the job. Some people have been known to refuse lifts because of it,' Lucas said. 'You can open a window if you like.'

'No, it's fine. I'll get used to it.' Libby pulled her seat-belt around her. The smell wasn't that bad after the initial shock. Sort of cleansing somehow. 'So where are we off to?'

'The other side of Pontivy,' Lucas said.

'Nice town,' Libby said, remembering a couple of occasions she and Dan had visited. 'I love the river there.'

'It is where I had my first job when I finish vetinaire school,' Lucas said. 'I enjoy my time there.'

Fields full of brilliant yellow rapeseed and pale blue flaxseed plants began to flash by as Lucas took the route nationale across country. Libby's favourite flower, the poppy, was waving around in the breeze too, adding its colour to the roadside hedges and verges.

'Thank you for taking the time and trouble to help me,' Libby said. 'I do appreciate it.'

Lucas shrugged. 'It's never a waste of time to help a friend. Beside, I like you and am happy to spend time with you.'

'Lucas, only a Frenchman would say that!'

Lucas looked puzzled. 'I am French!'

Libby laughed. 'Very!'

They were on the outskirts of Pontivy before Libby realised Lucas hadn't told her how much the car was, or even what make it was. She should have asked him before of course.

'This car — what make is it? And how much is it? How did you hear about it?'

Lucas answered the last question

first. 'It belongs to the wife of a friend. She is having a baby and needs a bigger car.'

'What sort is it?

'Italian.'

'A Fiat?'

'Non. An Alfa Romeo Spyder.'

'What? Oh Lucas, I should have said I don't have that much to spend on a car. An Alfa is sure to be too expensive and I'll have wasted your time.' Libby sank back down into her seat, frantically trying to remember what the few Alfa Romeos she'd ever seen had been like, but couldn't. All she could remember about them was Dan once saying they were superbly engineered.

'The car is not new and my friend she not ask a lot of money. I think you will like the car. I see you driving it,' Lucas said. 'It is the kind of car you should have.'

A minute later and Lucas turned down a lane and pulled to a stop outside a cottage with a garden full of roses and lots of colourful pots and hanging baskets everywhere.

'What a lovely cottage,' Libby said, watching as a pregnant woman opened the front door and made her way over to them.

'Lucas, darling. This is Libby? Welcome. I am Natalie. Come, I show you the car.' She led the way round the side of the cottage towards an outbuilding.

Parked in front of the building were three cars: a large four-by-four, an immaculate silver estate, and a scarlet two-seater sports car.

'This is Bella,' Natalie said, opening the sports-car door and handing Libby the keys. 'Take her for a drive. I'd come with you but I can't actually get in her anymore.'

Libby knew she was a lost cause the moment she sat in the driver's seat and turned the ignition on. She glanced across at Lucas as he slid into the passenger seat.

'I need a sensible grown-up car.'

'Why?'

'Why? Because, because . . . ' Libby's

voice trailed away. 'Because I'm a grown-up.'

'Not the correct answer,' Lucas laughed. 'Come on, drive.'

Driving around the lanes surrounding Natalie's house, Libby tried to rationalise her thoughts. This Spyder was only a two-seater — but did that matter now she was on her own? Or was she being silly even considering buying a sports car?

It was a lovely car to drive. She'd always wanted a sports car, particularly a red one, but there had never been a time in her life when it would have been practical to buy one. Besides, it had always been Dan who'd chosen their cars, and he'd gone for the sensible option every time.

'Sitting on the left and changing gear with my right hand is going to take some getting used to,' she said, stopping at a junction.

'Has to be easier than driving a right-hand car on the left though,' Lucas said. 'You'll soon get used to it.

You can at least see properly for over-taking — and reversing!'

'It is a dream to drive,' Libby said, deciding to ignore the comment about her reversing. 'I can just imagine driving with the roof down in summer too.'

Parking the car back at Natalie's, Libby sighed as she turned off the ignition. What to do? The car was beautiful. But was it the right car for her to buy?

'What did you mean earlier, saying it was the kind of car I should drive?' she asked, suddenly remembering Lucas's words.

'It's a very feminine car. Like you,' Lucas said quietly.

'Oh!' Not the reply she'd been expecting. 'But is it a sensible car for me to have?'

Lucas shrugged. 'Why do you have to have a sensible car? Is it not better to have one you like and enjoy driving?'

'I do like it a lot,' Libby said, stroking the steering wheel. 'OK, next question. How much is it?' After all, that would be the deciding factor. When Lucas told her the price she smiled at him in delight.

'Are you sure? That's under my budget! I can actually afford this car.'

'Re-registration will be a couple of hundred euros don't forget,' Lucas said. 'But the tyres are good and the control technique is new. I think it is a good buy.'

'Let's go find Natalie and tell her Bella has found herself a new owner,' Libby said, giving the steering wheel one last loving stroke and making her mind up. Who'd have thought she'd ever own a car called Bella?

★　★　★

'I've put you upstairs in the apartment with me,' Libby told Helen. 'Technically it's Chloe's room but she's not here, so . . . ' Libby shrugged as she looked at her sister-in-law. 'I thought you'd prefer to be up with me rather than downstairs in a guest room.'

'Definitely,' Helen said, following

Libby up the stairs. 'I'll just dump my stuff and then you can give me the guided tour.'

'The Bichets are in a couple of the rooms and Evie is in another, so I can't show you those, but the rest of the auberge is open for your inspection,' Libby said.

'I'm not sure I could take complete strangers into my home,' Helen said. 'Don't you think it's a bit of a risk?'

Libby laughed. 'Never thought about it. It's what auberges and B&Bs do. Besides, the Bichets have been coming here for years. Odette speaks very highly of them.'

'But this Evie. What do you know about her?'

'She's a guest — what do I need to know about her?' Libby glanced at Helen, puzzled. Evie was her friend now and no way would she hear a word against her, especially from someone who had yet to meet her.

'Isn't it a bit . . . well, chancy, letting complete strangers into your home?'

Helen said now. 'Foreign strangers. You never know what they might do. Murder you in your own bed and run off with the silver!'

Libby looked at her sister-in-law in astonishment. She hadn't been here five minutes and already she was questioning Libby's judgement like she had done so often in the past.

'Might do? Murder me? Oh Helen, I think you've been watching too many repeats of *Midsomer Murders*,' Libby laughed. 'Come on, let's do the guided tour bit and then we can go back down and have a cuppa. You'll meet everyone later and you'll see then how nice and ordinary everyone is. Not a closet killer amongst them.' It was going to be a long ten days if Helen continued to be so suspicious of everything and everybody.

'So tell me, how do you and Peter like having a teenager in the house?' Libby said once they were back downstairs in the communal sitting room. Her fingers were mentally crossed as she asked the question. Knowing how distressing Helen had found her inability to have children with Peter, she hoped it was all working out. It had taken Helen years to accept the situation and at one point she'd even refused to have friends with young children visit her. She just couldn't handle it. At one point she'd even told Libby to stop bringing Chloe with her for visits, refusing to look at any photographs until Chloe was at least eight years old.

Libby hoped having a grown-up Chloe living in her house for several weeks wouldn't drag up all the old regretted emotions for Helen.

'It's fun. Haven't seen a lot of her,' Helen said. 'It's long hours; she rarely gets back to us before eight or nine. She's definitely enjoying the job though, not to mention the social life.

'Chloe told you about her new boyfriend?' Helen asked.

'Didn't even know she had a new one,' Libby said now. 'Do tell.' She really missed having Chloe around and hearing about her new life face to face.

Chats on the phone or on Skype weren't the same, and besides, there hadn't been that many recently. Had she taken to confiding in Helen instead? Libby pushed a tiny tremor of jealousy away.

Helen shrugged. 'Not much to tell. He's someone she's met through work. I think his name is Alastair and he comes from Edinburgh. That's basically all I know.'

Chloe and Alastair had a good ring to it, but why hadn't Chloe mentioned him to her? After Dan's death they'd leant on each other for support and had grown close in the process. There had been times when Libby had thought their relationship was more akin to sisters than mother and daughter, especially when Chloe was being up-front with her about boyfriends and the things she and her friends got up to.

Libby sighed, hoping Helen wouldn't notice. She was as guilty as Chloe really. She'd stopped telling her about all the little day-to-day things that were happening in her life, just filling her in with the big events. Maybe if she'd stayed in the UK she and Chloe would still be chatting about the more personal events in their lives. Not that she had anything personal to tell Chloe.

It was silly to think things wouldn't change as Chloe became more independent. Inevitably she would meet somebody to love and spend her life with. Was it going to be this Alastair?

'She sounded pretty tired the other evening when she rang,' Libby said. 'Burning the proverbial candle at both ends by the sound of it.'

'We all did it at that age,' Helen said. 'And some of us fail to outgrow the habit.'

Libby looked at her. 'Peter?'

'Yes. Since his promotion he's been busier at work. He's chasing all over the country by day and then entertaining clients in the evenings. Can't tell you how many dinner parties I've had to go to, and organise, recently.'

'Can't you get him to slow down?

Remind him what happened to Dan,'
Libby said.

Helen shook her head, but before she
could reply a car horn being pressed in
a series of joyful toots sounded outside.

'That will be Lucas,' Libby said
excitedly. 'Come and meet him and see
my new car.'

When Lucas had offered to not only
help with the registration paperwork
but to also collect the car for her, Libby
had accepted gratefully.

'*Bonjour*, Lucas. *Ca va?*' Libby said
as Lucas greeted her with his now
customary kiss on the cheek.

'I am good, thank you,' Lucas
replied. 'And your car is good too.'

'She's even prettier than I remember,' Libby said, walking around the
car. 'I'm really looking forward to
driving her. Oh Lucas, meet my
sister-in-law Helen.'

'I have the papers for you to sign,'
Lucas said after shaking hands with
Helen. 'You have the green insurance
ticket for the windscreen?'

Libby nodded. 'It arrived yesterday.'

'*Bon*,' Lucas said, glancing at his watch. 'I will post the signed papers on my way to evening surgery.'

While Lucas spread the papers on the kitchen table, Libby fetched the envelope from the insurance company and handed it to him before making the coffee.

'Right. You need to sign this one and this one, initial this one, and sign this one,' Lucas said, handing her a pen. 'While you sign I'll just go and put the insurance ticket in the windscreen.'

'I know the French love their paperwork,' Libby laughed. 'But this is over the top!'

Lucas shrugged. 'It's normal. Everyone now has proof you own the car and it's a legal transaction.'

'I have to admit I'd never have found my way through all this paperwork. Can't thank you enough,' Libby said.

'Sure you can. You can take me for a drive and buy me a drink,' Lucas said, looking at her. 'I'm free most evenings after about seven.'

'Now there's an offer you can't refuse,' Helen said.

'Oh but I can,' Libby said lightly. 'Sorry, Lucas, but I've got evening meals to organise these days. Maybe when the summer is over? In the meantime how about I make you a cake instead? What's your favourite?'

'Chocolate. Not the same, but so long as you share it with me, I suppose it will have to do,' Lucas said, shaking his head at her, before going outside to the car.

Helen shook her head at her too. 'He's so nice. You should have agreed. Be good for you to have a man in your life again.'

'Right now getting this place up and running is enough. I don't need a man in my life,' Libby said. However attractive and helpful he might be. 'It would just complicate things.'

★ ★ ★

Libby and Helen carried some nibbles, a bottle of wine and two glasses down to the small teak table under the rose-covered pergola in the side garden overlooking the canal weir.

'I thought we'd indulge ourselves for half an hour before we start preparing dinner,' Libby said, pulling the cork out of the wine bottle and pouring two glasses.

'It's so peaceful here,' Helen said, taking a glass and settling herself in a chair. 'No traffic noise at all.'

'The tranquility is one of the things Dan and I loved most about this place,' Libby said. 'Also there does seem to be a certain magic here. *Santé*,' she added, picking up her own glass and clinking it with Helen's.

'Another thing I can't quite believe is how busy you are already,' Helen said.

Libby shrugged. 'That's still down to Odette really. She built up a good reputation over the years and most of the guests are regulars. The test will be next summer seeing if they return.'

'I know the Bichets are long-standing customers, but the family that arrived yesterday just appeared,' Helen said. 'They seem more than happy with what you offer.'

Libby smiled happily. So far people did seem to appreciate her style of hospitality. 'This evening when the Pauls arrive, I'll be full for the first time,' she said. 'I hope you don't mind being roped in to help? I feel I'm hijacking your holiday.'

'Don't be silly. I'm only too happy to help,' Helen said. 'But you're clearly going to need more help for the rest of the summer.'

Libby nodded. 'I already have someone from the village organised to start next month. Odette has promised to come and help this evening and tomorrow night.'

'So what are we cooking tonight?' Helen asked.

'Starters will be *les beignets de fleurs de courgettes*.'

'Oh, I loved those when you did

them for Peter and me that time,' Helen said. 'I'd never have dreamt courgette flowers could be so delicious.'

'The main course is cod with white wine sauce, served with asparagus and new potatoes. Followed by the obligatory cheese board, and then dessert is either tarte tatin or raspberries and fromage frais. Sound all right?' Libby asked.

'Sounds delicious. It's a good job I'm only here for ten days,' Helen said. 'As it is, I'll be dieting for the next month when I get home.'

They both turned, hearing a car stop in the auberge parking area. 'Better go see who that is,' Libby said, standing up. To her surprise, Odette got out of the car with two people she'd never seen before.

'Libby, this is Kevin and Tracey Chambers. They need your help. Been badly let down with their house purchase and need somewhere to stay while it resolves itself. Three nights at the most.'

'What's happened?' Libby asked as

she shook hands with the couple.

'They've come over to complete the purchase today and move into the cottage over Spezet way tonight. But the vendor is declining to let them have access to water and electricity. The notaire says they can't complete until he's sorted it in their favour. He's promised it will be finalised by the weekend, but in the meantime they need somewhere to stay.'

'I'm so sorry,' Libby said. 'I can't help. I have guests arriving this evening for the last available room. I'm full for the next week.' She turned to Odette. 'Do you know anyone else who could maybe help?'

Odette shook her head. 'Everywhere, like you, is full.' She glanced at Libby. 'What about the gîte? You've got that ready, haven't you?'

'It's clean and tidy but I haven't decorated yet. But yes, it's empty. You are welcome to stay in it until you move into your cottage if that helps,' she said.

'Thank you,' Tracey said. 'You're a life-saver.'

'I'll get the key and some bedding,' Libby said.

Helen volunteered to make up the gîte bed and see to anything else that needed doing to make the place 'guest-ready', while Libby and Odette started dinner preparations in the auberge.

Beating the batter for the courgette starter, Libby looked across at Odette. 'You OK? You look a bit tired.'

Odette sighed. 'I tell you Isabelle come soon?'

'You must be looking forward to that,' Libby said.

'*Oui* and *non*. I do not understand why she come alone. Bruno think maybe she and Laurent are having problems.' Odette rinsed the salad and rocket leaves that were to accompany the courgette flowers and spun them vigorously in the salad drainer. 'I try to ring her the other night but there was no reply.'

'Laurent is probably too busy with work,' Libby said, remembering how happy Isabelle and Laurent had been on their wedding day seven years ago. Their wedding — the only French one she and Dan had ever been to — had been such a joyful affair. The whole village had celebrated with the happy couple, and Isabelle had been so vivacious she'd positively radiated with happiness that day.

'Perhaps. He is responsible for several people now,' Odette said. 'He works long hours, I know.' She began to scrub the new potatoes ready for cooking. 'I try not to worry but I can't stop. Perhaps I need more to do.'

'Well, you know you're more than welcome to help me up here,' Libby said, glad to be given an opportunity to change the subject. Nothing she could say would stop Odette worrying until she could talk to Isabelle face to face. 'Extra hands are always welcome.' And having Odette around to help her regularly would have been ideal.

'Bruno, he keeps talking about going away on *vacances*.'

'A holiday somewhere warm could be

just what you need. Are you still thinking about starting a monthly luncheon club?'

Odette nodded. 'Yes, but I think I wait until after the summer. September would be good.' She paused. 'I know then, too, what is going on with Isabelle.'

For several moments they worked in companionable silence, Libby making the tarte tatin and Odette preparing the asparagus before placing it in the steamer.

'Libby, could I have a word please?' Evie asked, standing in the kitchen doorway.

Libby looked around in surprise. 'Sure. Coffee?'

Evie shook her head. 'No, thanks. It's about my stay here.'

'You want to check out?'

'No, no. The opposite. I want to stay for the summer. But not in the auberge. I would like to rent the gîte from you.'

'Oh! Evie, I'm sorry. There are two people moving into it right now.'

'How long are they staying?' Evie

asked, disappointed.

'Three days, they think.'

'After that, could I rent it for the rest of the summer?'

'I suppose so,' Libby said. 'But I thought you had to get back to Paris soon?'

Evie shrugged. 'Not necessarily, although if I can't move into the gîte right away, I think I'll perhaps take the opportunity to go up for a quick visit to sort a few things out and to collect some extra clothes and bits and pieces I'll need for a longer stay.'

'I'm so glad you will be staying here for the summer,' Libby said, smiling at Evie. 'I'll make sure the gîte is ready for you to move into when you get back.'

9

Suzette

Suzette stood on the small balcony of her apartment, looking down at the Paris traffic. Normally when she returned from being away she was relieved to be back and stood here to soak up the frenzy of the City of Lights contentedly, knowing she was home. But today, for some reason, the magic simply wasn't there.

Today the rue looked unkempt, with litter blowing about in the breeze, and somehow the noise and bustle of people and the city traffic with its loud hooters and sirens made everything feel belligerent — as if everyone was personally fighting a war of survival. Suzette sighed. How was it possible things had changed so much?

This was silly. It was her home. She

only felt unsettled because of the changes she knew she was facing in her life. A long holiday in the countryside would surely help her in deciding which way her future lay, but it was to this apartment she'd have to return at the end of summer to begin her new life.

Resolutely, Suzette went inside and closed the French windows. She had two whole days ahead of her with lots of things planned and she was determined to make the most of it.

She made her way to the bedroom cupboard and took out a suitcase. Might as well make a start on packing a few things. Shoes and clothes first. And some material and embroidery silks. The cape with its intricate Lesage tribute she'd been working on before Monaco was finally finished and she was itching to start something else.

Infuriatingly, she couldn't find anything in the pile of new material she kept in her sewing cupboard that inspired her. At least she now had an excuse to go to the Marché Saint-Pierre tomorrow and see what treasures she could find.

With the suitcase already half full, Suzette decided to leave the packing until she'd done the shopping she planned to do. At this rate if she wasn't careful she'd end up having to take two suitcases back to the auberge.

Suzette was up early the next day, and after nipping out for a croissant and coffee which she ate sitting on the balcony, she got ready for a happy few hours wandering around her two favourite markets. First up would be the textile market.

Suzette loved choosing material at the Marché Saint-Pierre. So many shops and bazaars full of a variety of her favourite materials — velvets, linen and silks to name but three.

Today she even loved the time-consuming business of actually buying some fabric in the large store that bore the market's name; first find a bolt of the material you wanted, then find an assistant to cut it for you and hand you a bill; find the cash desk, pay and then return to the same assistant to claim your purchase. It would have been easier to shop in one of the many smaller outlets but she'd fallen totally in love with some stunning scarlet velvet material she planned to use as a base for some cushion covers.

Standing waiting to pay for the several pieces of material she'd chosen, she picked up a leaflet advertising the Fête des Brodeuses, Pont-l'Abbé, Bretagne. Thoughtfully Suzette placed it in the bag with her purchases. Pont l'Abbé wasn't far from the auberge. An exhibition of embroidery and costumes sounded interesting and might give her some design ideas for her own work.

It was nearly lunchtime before Suzette had completed her material purchases, so she hailed a cab to take her to the Marché les Enfants Rouges where she intended to indulge in one of her favourite meals, cornet vegetarian, prepared by one of the market's regular stall-holders.

Waiting and watching as her favourite galette was being cooked and filled, she began to exchange her usual banter with the cook. To her surprise, while he was friendly enough, he didn't really engage with her like he usually did.

It wasn't until she was sat eating her salad-filled galette that she realised why. He hadn't recognised her. She was wearing her Evie wig. As far as he was concerned she was just a passing customer, not one of his regulars. Suzette smiled to herself. She was beginning to enjoy going incognito. It certainly made a change from being asked for her autograph whenever she was recognised.

Once back in the apartment Suzette placed the materials in the case, along with some candles she'd been unable to resist in the Marché les Enfants Rouge. Then, after pouring herself a glass of wine, she stepped out onto the balcony with a happy sigh. Once she'd become acclimatised again to the hustle and bustle of city life, she'd enjoyed herself.

She was looking forward, though, to getting back to Brittany and the peace and quiet that surrounded the auberge.

Later she'd go downstairs with a large stamped envelope and ask the concierge to forward her post to Brittany for the next couple of months. She'd need to swear him to secrecy and make him promise not to give out the address to anyone. A bribe of a larger Christmas bonus than usual should do the trick.

Later that evening as she was finishing her packing ready to leave in the morning, her mobile rang. Suzette answered it without even glancing at the caller ID. She knew instinctively it was Malik.

'You are talking to me then,' he said. 'How's country life?'

'Actually I've been in Paris for the past few days,' Suzette said. 'I needed to pick some things up.'

'Haven't changed your mind about hibernating for the summer then?'

'No.'

'I'm back late on Monday. Any chance you'll still be around?'

'Afraid not,' Suzette said. 'I'm off early tomorrow. How did Geneva go? Sponsorship deal going ahead?'

'One or two little details to sort but yes, all will be signed by the end of the week.'

'I'm pleased for you,' Suzette said. 'Can you say more or is it still hush-hush?'

'I'll tell you all about it when we next see each other,' Malik said. 'Any idea when that's likely to be?'

'*Non*. A couple of weeks,' Suzette said. She heard Malik sigh.

'Rehearsals for *Swan Lake* will start first week in September so you'd better be back by then. You are exercising and at least doing some barre work, aren't you?'

Suzette heard the anxiety in his voice. 'Yes, I'm exercising.' No point in mentioning she'd been neglecting her barre work. When she got back to the gîte it was one of the things she intended to sort. There was more room there and she should be able to fix up some sort of temporary barre to work with. Whether her ankle was ready to start exercising again was something she didn't want to even think about yet.

'I'll phone you next week to see how you are,' Malik said. 'Please answer. Promise me no more ignoring my calls.'

'I promise,' Suzette said. 'Just don't hound me. I really and truly need the time and space to decide what the future holds for me.'

10

Libby

Libby had to admit that having Helen around to help with the routine auberge chores was a big help. With so many breakfasts to prepare, serve and clear up afterwards though, it was nearly eleven o'clock Sunday morning before Libby was able to begin to relax for the day. She'd promised to show Helen around a local beauty spot, followed by lunch at a riverside restaurant.

The sight of the sun trying to break through the clouds just as they were leaving for Châteauneuf-du-Faou Libby took as an auspicious sign and folded down the roof on her car before they set off.

'This holiday has gone so quickly,' Helen said as Libby negotiated one of the many bends on the road leading down to the small town.

'That's probably because I've been working you so hard,' Libby said. 'I'm sorry.'

'No. It's been fun. I've enjoyed every minute of it. It's a beautiful part of France. Oh, look at that chateau across the valley,' Helen said. 'It's pink.'

Libby laughed. 'That's Trévarez, known locally as the Pink Chateau for obvious reasons. Don't think we've got time to go there today. Next time you're over we'll go. You'll love exploring the grounds. Peter would be interested in the chateau's wartime history too I think.'

Libby parked in the centre of the small town and they had a coffee at a flower-decorated pavement café before returning to the car and heading down the long hill to the river. Before starting their walk alongside the river, Libby booked a table for lunch at one of the waterside restaurants.

'Right, let's work up an appetite,' she said, moving to one side of the path to let a woman with two excited border collies on leads pass. 'We'll go this way.'

They stopped to watch a group of young boys launch their canoes and, with lots of encouraging shouts to each other, begin to head upstream. They stood there for a few moments, letting two cyclists and a jogger pass before moving on. As the path followed the river and wound away from the houses they heard a series of barks and yapping in a field bordering the path. A large notice by the entrance proclaimed it to be a dog training session.

A dozen or so people were standing in a long line, all with a dog at their side. One by one the dogs were paraded up and down the line in an effort to try and convince the instructor they were well behaved.

'Isn't that your vet boyfriend?' Helen asked, indicating the instructor, who was standing apart from the line watching and occasionally offering a quiet word of advice. 'I think he's got quite a fan club going there with women of a certain age. There isn't another man in sight.'

Libby nodded. 'Yes, it's Lucas. But he's not my boyfriend.'

'Well he did ask you out,' Helen said. 'I still can't understand why you didn't accept.'

'Like I told you and him, I'm too busy.' Libby laughed as a young border collie slipped its collar and made straight for Lucas, jumping up and down and running around him.

'I'd love a dog again,' she said, watching the collie and remembering Tess the dog who'd been a part of their family for over fourteen years. She, Chloe and Dan had all been devastated when Tess had died, just six months before Dan himself.

'Maybe I'll look out for one when summer is over and I've got time.'

'Then you can join this class and Lucas can help you train it,' Helen teased her. 'Look, he's seen us.'

Acknowledging Lucas's wave with

one of her own and a friendly smile, Libby said, 'Come on, let's leave them to it and get back to the restaurant.' She wished Helen would stop going on about her getting together with Lucas. As far as she was concerned that was a definite no-no, although she was grateful for his help with the car.

If she did get a dog in a few months, she'd train it herself. No way would she join this Sunday-morning fan club of his.

Twenty minutes later they were sitting at their table, glasses of rosé in hand, studying the menu. Helen looked at Libby. 'It's good to see you looking happy again. You are happy, aren't you? I mean I know you miss Chloe and Dan of course, but you're building a new life for yourself here.' Helen sighed. 'I'm quite envious actually.'

'Envious? Oh Helen, please don't be. Yes I am happy here, but I still miss Dan. I'd love it to be the two of us running the auberge, living our dream together.' She glanced at Helen. 'Promise me when you get back you'll talk to Peter. Get him to take things easier. You need to start living whatever dreams the two of you have before it's too late. Like it was for Dan and me.'

11

Odette

Odette was at the bottom of her garden, creating a small border and planting some bedding plants around the olive tree, when Isabelle arrived. Delighted to see her, she stood up to give her a hug before stepping back and looking at her. 'You look well,' she said. 'Positively blooming. How is Laurent? I am so sorry he hasn't come with you.'

'He's fine. Just very busy at work. He sends his love.'

Odette smiled. 'You were very mysterious on the phone with Bruno. What's this visit all about?' She didn't mention the phone calls that had gone unanswered. The quicker they got any bad news out of the way the better, but Isabelle shook her head.

'Later. I need to talk to you both.

This garden will be amazing when you've finished,' she said, looking around.

'Thank you,' Odette said, stifling a sigh. Needing to talk to them both didn't bode well. 'Come on, let's go and get you settled in. I've put you in the big room at the back that used to be Grandma's. I hope you like it.'

'It's weird coming here and not to the auberge,' Isabelle said as they made their way up the stairs. 'I nearly gave the taxi driver the wrong address. Are you settled and happy here now? And how's Libby coping at the auberge?'

'Libby's well. I couldn't have sold to a better person. She has a full house this week and is loving it,' Odette said. 'And yes, I think I'm settled and happy here now.' Whether she was to remain happy or not depended on what Isabelle wanted to talk about.

It wasn't until later that evening when they were all sitting around the table under the loggia having dinner that Isabelle finally broached the subject of her visit, and that was only after Bruno had asked.

'So, *ma petite*, why are you here? And more importantly, why are you here alone?'

Odette held her breath, waiting for Isabelle to reply.

'It's Laurent,' Isabelle began. 'He's been promoted at work and will be doing a lot more travelling — Italy, Angleterre and even India on occasions. He'll be away for weeks at a time.'

Odette watched her as she fiddled nervously with the salad on her plate. So did Laurent's absence on business mean that Isabelle was giving up on her marriage?

'Are you and Laurent separating?' Odette demanded. She couldn't bear the suspense a moment longer.

'*Non!* Whatever gave you that idea? It's just that Laurent's work HQ will be based in Paris now, so even when he is not travelling he will have to spend his time there and not in Nice.

'So we've — or rather I've — decided,

and Laurent has agreed, that I'm going to move back to Bretagne rather than stay down south alone for weeks at a time. He knows I've never really settled down there; that I would prefer to be near family.'

Odette let out a huge sigh of relief.

'Where are you going to live?' Bruno asked.

'That's why I've come up — to start looking for a house and to ask a favour.' She took a deep breath. 'Can we — well, it will be mainly me on my own at first — please live with you for a few months while I find somewhere?'

'Oh I don't know about that,' Bruno said with a straight face. 'Your mama and I have got used to being alone.'

'Bruno, stop it this minute!' Odette said. 'Now is not the time to tease.' She smiled as she looked at Isabelle. 'I can't think of anything we'd like better. Of course you can stay here while you house-hunt. Stay as long as you like.'

'Your mama is right,' Bruno said. 'It will be like old times having you here.

How long are you staying this visit?'

'Laurent is in Italy at the moment, due back next week. I'll need to be back home by then, so about five days. I'm going to start registering with local estate agents and begin to find out what's available.

'There is one more thing,' Isabelle said, looking at Odette. 'I'm hoping to persuade you to come down south for a few days and help me pack up the house ready for moving. I could do with the help.'

'We could both come and have a *vacances* at the same time,' Bruno said.

Odette looked at him. A *vacances*. Didn't he remember just how much work was involved in moving just from the auberge to here? A holiday it wasn't. And Nice was a thousand kilometres away.

'What?' Bruno said, seeing the expression on her face.

'Surely you remember how stressful moving is?' she said.

'Well we could go down early and

have a few days' holiday before starting the packing. We could both do with some sun.'

'It's a great idea, Dad,' Isabelle said. 'Come back with me and I can show you Antibes, Cannes and Monaco — all the fun places — before we start packing the house up.'

'It would be our first summer holiday in I don't know how many years,' Bruno said thoughtfully. 'We've never had the opportunity to go down south in the summer before. You were always busy, with the auberge being so popular.'

Odette looked at him. Had he really missed going away for summer holidays because she was so busy with the auberge? He'd always seemed happy with the various long weekends they'd taken — usually in winter, she had to admit.

And Isabelle? Intuition told her that Isabelle wasn't telling them the full story behind her desire to come back home. Maybe over the next few days she'd relax and share the rest of her news.

'*D'accord*. I give in.' Odette smiled. 'We will have a family holiday before the hard work starts.'

'*Bon*. That's settled,' Bruno said. 'A *vacances* in the south of France. It will do us good.'

12

Libby

'Are you sure you don't mind helping me clean the gîte? It is the last day of your holiday,' Libby asked Helen.

With their house purchase finally sorted, the Chapmans had gone and Libby needed to clean and prepare the gîte ready for Evie's return. 'I still feel as though I'm imposing on you.'

'Don't be silly,' Helen said. 'I've got the reward of an hour or two at the village fête this afternoon to look forward to.'

Between the two of them, the gîte was quickly sparkling clean and the perfume from the vase of roses and lavender Libby placed in the sitting room began to waft through the small cottage.

'Are you going to transfer Evie's belongings over from the auberge?' Helen asked.

Libby shook her head. 'No. I did think about it but decided against. She might take it as an invasion of her privacy. I'll offer to give her a hand if she wants me to when she gets back.'

A horn tooted outside. '*La Poste*,' Libby said. Amongst the usual collection of promotion material there was a letter addressed to Evie.

'Strange. It's got a local postmark. Didn't think Evie knew anyone locally,' Libby said, propping it up against the vase of flowers after glancing at it curiously. 'Right, lunch and then it's fête time.'

Walking into the village Helen said, 'I'm so looking forward to bringing Peter here at the end of summer. You planning anything special for your birthday?'

'Don't think so,' Libby said. 'To be honest I'm not looking forward to the big four-oh. I'd far rather ignore it.'

'I think Chloe will insist you have a party — and actually so do I! Come on, Libby, you must celebrate. It's an important milestone in life!'

'Well with you, Peter and Chloe here

168

I'm sure we'll manage to crack a bottle of champagne, if not have an actual party,' Libby said.

The fête, held in the village picnic area down by the canal, was in full swing when they arrived, with music blaring out from the loudspeakers placed either side of a temporary stage where a group of musicians were performing. A large circle of people, hands linked, were dancing a traditional Breton dance in front of it, whilst onlookers clapped their encouragement.

Libby and Helen made their way over to Odette and Bruno, who were standing by the crêpe stall enjoying a coffee while they watched the dancing.

'Isabelle not with you?' Libby asked, disappointed. She'd been looking forward to catching up and hearing all her news.

'But yes,' Odette said, pointing to the dancers. 'There she is. It's as if she's never been away.'

'How is she?' Libby asked. 'Everything all right?'

Odette nodded happily. 'Yes.' Quickly she explained to Libby about Laurent's promotion and Isabelle's decision to move back. 'We're going down next week to help her pack. But before, we also have a short holiday in Nice.'

As the song the musicians were playing came to an end, Isabelle accompanied by Lucas left the circle and came across to join them.

'Libby, how nice to see you here. Come on, let me teach you Breton dancing.' And before she realised it, Lucas had taken her by the hand and was leading her towards the circle of dancers as the music started up again.

'Lucas, I ca — '

'You'll soon pick it up,' he assured her. 'It's very easy. Just watch and follow my steps. It's very repetitive.'

Libby smiled and gave in. 'OK.'

As Lucas's hand tightened around hers, she took hold of the hand of the woman on the other side of her; and as the music started she joined in with enthusiasm.

A few minutes later, as Libby was happily stepping and swinging, Lucas glanced at her. 'Something tells me you've done this before, haven't you?'

'Odette taught me years ago,' Libby admitted. 'Dan never liked dancing, but as you don't need a partner for this I could just join in with the crowd.'

'And there was me thinking I could teach you,' Lucas sighed.

Libby shook her head when at the end of the dance he asked, 'Again?'

'Maybe later when I've got my breath back. I hadn't realised I was so unfit.'

Looking around for Helen, Libby saw that she, Odette and Isabelle had managed to secure a picnic table in the shade. 'Shall we join Helen and the others in the shade over there?'

As he strolled alongside her, Lucas asked, 'Do you like jazz?'

'Some of it,' Libby said. 'I'm not that keen on modern stuff; I prefer the traditional. Proper jazz and swing.'

'There's a group of us planning to go to the local jazz fest one evening. Would you like me to get you a ticket? It's down by the river and is usually good fun, a mix of modern and traditional jazz.'

Libby hesitated. Going with Lucas and a group of people couldn't be construed as a date, could it? She liked Lucas a lot and she did need to expand her social life. Maybe some of his friends would, in time, become her friends too. But she didn't want him to think it was a date.

'Thank you. I'll look forward to it. Let me know how much the ticket is and I'll — '

Lucas interrupted her and shook his head. 'No need. My treat.'

Helen overheard the words 'my treat' and looked at her questioningly, but before she could say anything Bruno and Pascal appeared carrying trays of cold drinks.

'Left the pepineré in safe hands this afternoon then?' Lucas asked, accepting a lager from Pascal.

'I think most of my customers are

down here, so I'm not expecting a lot of sales,' Pascal said. 'Besides, with Mother opening this, there was no way I was going to be allowed to miss it.'

'Where's your mother now?' Libby asked. She'd heard much about Pascal's matriarch of a mother but had never seen her in person.

'I'm afraid you've missed her. The heat this year is too much for her so once she'd cut the ribbon, declared the fête open and watched the first dance, she took a taxi home.'

'Talking of home,' Helen said, glancing at her watch, 'I'm going to have to make tracks if I'm to catch the evening ferry.'

'And I've got to get tonight's evening meal organised,' Libby said, regretfully getting to her feet.

'Are you full this week?' Pascal asked.

'All the rooms are taken but not everyone is having dinner tonight, and of course Evie isn't here — not that she eats a proper dinner regularly. So it's just dinner for seven today.'

'Has Evie checked out?' Pascal asked.

Libby shook her head. 'No, the opposite. She's decided to rent the gîte for the rest of summer and has hared off to Paris to pick up some more of her things. Right,' she said, 'thanks for the drink. Helen and I are off. Isabelle, we must catch up later.'

Walking back to the auberge, Helen said, 'So you've got a 'treat' arranged with Lucas then?'

'Seems like it,' Libby said. 'I'm spending the evening with him and a group of his friends at the jazz festival,' she added, knowing that Helen would keep probing until she told her.

'Sounds like a date to me,' Helen said.

'Hardly a date with so many people,' Libby said as her mobile rang. Chloe. 'Darling, how are you?'

'I'm fine. Is Aunty Helen still with you?'

'Leaving in ten minutes.'

'I need you to ask her to do me a favour,' Chloe said. 'Alastair has invited me to his end-of-term undergraduate do and I need my ball dress; I can't afford to buy another one. It's in the wardrobe in my room if she can please bring it back with her.'

'Shouldn't be a problem,' Libby said. 'So this Alastair is a student then? Not someone you work with.'

'He's a third-year medical student and I'll tell you all about him when I come home, Mum, so stop fishing. Sorry, I've got to go. I'm phoning from work. Thank Aunty Helen for me and tell her I'll have the kettle on when she gets back. *Ciao*.'

'*Ciao*,' Libby echoed. No mention of actually bringing Alastair to meet her. Just, she'd be told about him. Libby sighed as she turned to Helen.

'You have an urgently needed ball gown to take back with you, if that's OK. Alastair is taking her to his university ball.'

'No problem,' Helen said. 'And don't worry; if — when — I get to meet this Alastair, I'll phone you straight away with all the details.'

13

Evie

Evie settled back into her seat with a sigh of contentment as the train pulled out of the Paris station. The weekend had been good but now she was glad to be leaving. A couple more hours and the heat and bustle of the city would be behind her and she'd be back in the quiet countryside of Brittany to enjoy the summer on her own terms.

It was good that Malik had at last accepted her decision to disappear for the summer. She knew so long as she spoke to him on the phone regularly, promised to keep exercising and be back in Paris for September, he'd stop worrying. Sitting there as the train gathered speed and hurtled past vineyards and then fields of sunflowers before finally reaching the large artichoke fields of

Brittany, Evie let her thoughts drift.

She had so many plans for 'Evie' to enjoy a normal life for the next couple of months. She'd get involved in village life, visit the coast, wander around the exhibition at Pont-l'Abbé, make friends with Libby. And all the time she'd be incognito, enjoying just being herself.

Evie even had the germ of a tentative, exciting idea about where her future could lay. Researching its feasibility would be easier without the pressure of people asking all the time, 'But what will you do without dancing?'

It was late afternoon when her taxi from the station pulled up outside the auberge. As the driver got the two bulging suitcases out of the boot, Libby appeared.

'Evie. Welcome back. The gîte is all ready for you. Gosh, however did you manage one case, let alone two?' she said, struggling to pick up the smaller one. 'This weighs a ton.'

'With difficulty,' Evie admitted. 'But there was so much I thought I might need.' If she was truthful too, she was trying to avoid the possibility of having to return to Paris again before she was ready, to collect some item that suddenly became indispensable in the coming weeks.

Setting the suitcase down in the sitting room Libby said, 'I'll leave you to unpack and settle in. Dinner's at the usual time, if you'd like some?'

Evie shook her head. 'I won't bother tonight, thanks. I'll get on with things in here.'

'I've put a few things in the fridge for you if you get desperate,' Libby said. 'Before I forget — I left your clothes and other things in your bedroom in the auberge. If you'd like a hand moving them over, just ask.'

Once on her own in the gîte, Evie opened the suitcases and set about turning her temporary home into her own space: a large cream throw over the settee, a couple of her red velvet embroidered cushions strategically placed, perfumed candles on the coffee table, her favourite pillow on the bed. Books and photographs on the bookshelves, her laptop on the kitchen table plugged in and charging. She placed a round pink stone floor light in the corner at the foot of the stairs and switched it on before looking around her with satisfaction. She'd even managed to make a small space to do some barre work by tying the handle of the broom between two chairs. Not ideal, and there was no mirror, but it would be good enough for her to at least start practising movements again.

It was only then that she noticed the envelope Libby had propped against the vase of flowers in the sitting room. Curiously Evie looked at it. Madame Evie Patem. None of her Parisian friends knew where she was, or the fact that she was here incognito, so who could it possibly be from?

Carefully she opened it and pulled out a glossy black-and-white postcard photograph of the old village school circa 1900. She turned it over and read the message scrawled on the back. And smiled. An invitation to dinner from an unexpected source. A telephone number to ring if she wanted to accept. If she didn't ring it would be understood she'd declined the invitation and there would be no hard feelings.

Thoughtfully Evie placed the postcard on the table. To go or not to go? She'd think about it while she finished emptying the suitcases of her clothes and hung them in the wardrobe.

An hour later and everything was in place. Now to get her remaining things from the auberge bedroom. The front door was open and hearing the authoritative voice of a TV news presenter coming from the direction of the sitting room, Evie went in search of Libby.

About to gently knock the sitting-room door before walking in, she froze as she heard, 'Mystery surrounds the disappearance of ballerina Suzette Shelby from Monaco after incurring another injury during rehearsals. Sources close to Suzette say they are worried as it is completely out of character.'

Evie held her breath as she waited for

the news presenter to say more, but as a brief clip of Suzette dancing faded away, he switched to the next story.

A voice Evie didn't recognise said, 'Surprised it's taken this long for the media to pick up on this story. Everyone down south was talking about it before I came up. Apparently she's hugely depressed over the amount of injuries she's had these last couple of seasons and knows it signals the end of her career.'

'Must be hard though,' Libby answered. 'Having to give up a career like that which has been your whole life. Bit like footballers really; they pass their sell-by date at a young age.'

Evie wanted to scream out, 'It's nothing like footballers. Top professional ones earn scandalous amounts of money — unlike me! I still have to earn a living.'

Instead she took a deep breath and walking into the room saying, 'Hi, Libby. I've come over to collect my things from the bedroom. I expect you'd like to be able to get it ready for more guests.'

Libby stood up and quickly introduced Evie to Isabelle. 'Odette's daughter. Can I give you a hand moving things?'

Evie shook her head. 'There's not much to do. I'll be fine. Enjoy the rest of your evening.' She went quickly upstairs to her old room.

Gathering together the clothes she'd left hanging in the wardrobe and a couple of books from the bedside table, Evie checked that she'd picked up everything and took it all back to the gîte.

Once it was all put away she sank down onto the settee and allowed herself to think about being a news item on national TV. Who exactly were these 'sources close to her' who were worried? They only needed to talk to Malik and surely he would set their minds at rest without divulging where she was.

Next time she spoke to him she'd suggest he told anybody who was still interested that while he didn't know where she was, they were in contact and everything was fine. The media would soon get bored then, with nothing salacious to feed their curiosity.

Evie picked up the postcard from the table and reread the message. To accept or not? Why not? Now she was staying here for the summer, it would be good to get out and about and make new friends. She tapped out the number on her mobile and listened to its ringing tone.

'Hello. This is Evie Patem. I would be delighted to have dinner with you one evening.'

14

Libby

Libby put the final touches on the cake she'd promised to make Lucas and stood back to look at it. Cake decoration had never been a skill of hers so she'd simply covered it with an easily made chocolate ganache. It certainly looked good enough to eat.

She glanced at the kitchen clock. Evening surgery would be finishing about now. She'd give Lucas a ring and see if he wanted to collect the cake on his way home. An unusual noise sounded outside as she went to pick up the phone and she hesitated, listening. Silence.

She dialled the surgery number and waited. Just as Lucas answered the noise sounded again.

'Hi. The cake I promised you is ready, if you'd like to collect it tonight?'

There was that noise again. Louder this time. Definitely an animal in pain. She'd have to investigate. 'Sorry, Lucas; I'll ring you back. There's something going on outside.'

She hung up and grabbing a jacket from the cupboard, ran outside.

Which direction was the noise coming from? She checked the chickens and the ducks before walking quickly down onto the canal path. The noise sounded again and appeared to be coming from a field bordering the canal path 50 yards away.

Libby began to run down the path wishing she'd thought to pick up her mobile phone. She had no way of calling for assistance if she needed it. If only the Bichets had been around in the auberge — Andre in particular. She was sure he'd have joined her on her mission. But the Bichets had elected to go to the cinema in the nearby town and didn't expect to be back before eleven o'clock.

It would be dusk soon, which would

make seeing and finding any injured animal more difficult. As she ran she heard a car coming down the canal path behind her. She turned and sighed in relief as she recognised the car. Lucas.

'I heard the noise down the phone and thought you might need a hand.' Taking a large industrial-sized torch from the front seat, he slammed the car door shut.

'Whatever it is seems to be in that field there,' Libby said, pointing to the field on their left. As they made their way into the field another pitiful cry filled the evening air, and Lucas switched on the torch and shone the light around the field.

'There it is.'

Halfway up the field a young fawn had somehow got caught up in some orange electric fence netting the farmer had placed across the field opening. Every time the fence pulsed he cried. Ten yards away a doe was watching.

'Right, I need to get some things from the car. Wait here.' He ran back down to the path. A minute later he was back with three thick rubber gloves and a large wooden-handled knife.

'If we go this way we should be able to get to him,' Lucas said, starting up a small track alongside the hedge. Heart in mouth, Libby followed him.

'I can't see why the farmer has left this fence on. There aren't any animals in the field. Unfortunately I can't see anywhere to switch the damn thing off. Luckily he's this side, so we can at least reach him,' Lucas said. He handed Libby the torch. 'I think I can manage without light. It will only distress him more, shining in his eyes.'

Quickly he pulled on two of the industrial black rubber gloves and wrapped the third around the knife's wooden handle. Kneeling down beside the distressed animal, he murmured quietly as he stroked it gently, trying to work out the best way to do things.

Somehow the fawn had got his head through one of the small squares of the mesh netting but couldn't pull it back.

Working between the regular pings of electricity and talking softly, Lucas quickly cut the mesh in several places.

Libby could see that Lucas, although somewhat protected by the rubber gloves, was also receiving a short shock with each cut he made, but it took less than ten seconds to make the hole big enough and he was able to gently pull the fawn's head back through the opened-up space.

The poor animal was exhausted. Gently Lucas picked him up and carried him into a corner of the field before laying him down on clear ground under the shelter of a hedge. 'Goodness only knows how long he's been there,' he said. 'If we move away the doe should go to him.'

'I don't think he can have been there more than half an hour,' Libby said thoughtfully. 'I only heard his cries as I rang you.

'Are you OK?' Libby asked as Lucas peeled off the rubber gloves.

'I'm fine. Didn't get too many

shocks. These definitely protected me.'

Together they stood in the shadows watching as the doe made her way to the fawn and started to nuzzle him.

'D'you think he'll be all right?' Libby whispered.

Lucas nodded. 'I think we got here just in time. Let's leave him to his mum. We'll come back later and check on him.'

Back at the auberge, Libby made some coffee. Lucas, after admiring the cake, insisted she share a slice with him.

'You are still coming to the jazz down in Chateauneuf? I picked up the tickets today,' Lucas said.

'Definitely. I'm looking forward to it,' Libby replied. 'And to meeting your friends.'

'How's your daughter? Enjoying her job?' Lucas asked.

Libby nodded. 'She seems to be doing really well. She's promised to come over soon but I'm not holding my breath.' Libby sighed. 'She's really busy at work and now she's got a boyfriend, her social life has also taken off.' She glanced at Lucas. 'D'you have any children?'

'Never been married, so no. I have a niece and a nephew though, both about to start uni. My sister is already fretting about them leaving home.'

'I know how she feels,' Libby said.

'Luckily she's got our mother living nearby,' Lucas said. 'She'll make sure she doesn't have time on her hands.'

'Whereabouts in France do they live?'

'Bordeaux,' Lucas said. 'My parents moved there when they retired to be near Veronique and her family. I was busy being a locum here, there and everywhere and basically had no idea where I was going to end up.'

'Where are you from originally?'

'Paris. But for the last twenty-odd years I've lived all over France — Burgundy, Dordogne, Provence, the lot, and now here I am up in Brittany. I finally managed to set up my own practice.'

'Does that mean you're settled up

here for good?' Libby asked. 'Or do you plan to build up the business and sell it on? I should imagine it's very different to all those other French departments, especially the south-of-France ones.'

Lucas cut another slice of cake and offered it to Libby. When she shook her head he put it on his own plate.

'Sell up? No, I don't think so. After the crowds of the south — all those tourists — it's wonderful here,' he said. 'Mind you, I do miss the wall-to-wall sunshine, but I'd had my fill of over-pampered pets. Now I've got a real mixture of animals to deal with — domestic, farm and even the occasional wild one. Which reminds me. We'd better go and check up on our fawn.' Lucas looked at his watch. 'He's had long enough to recover now, I think.'

Libby glanced up at the kitchen clock. She'd lost track of time chatting to Lucas and was surprised to see it was over an hour since Lucas had pulled the fawn out of the fence.

Dusk had given way to darkness and

this time they did need the torch as they made their way along the canal path. Silently they turned into the field and Lucas shone the torch to where he'd left the young fawn.

There was no sign of either him or the doe. 'Good,' Lucas said. 'Mum has obviously taken him off somewhere safer.'

Walking back to the auberge, Libby missed her footing in a pot-hole and would have fallen if Lucas hadn't grabbed her and then taken her by the hand.

'Thanks.'

Lucas didn't answer. He didn't let go of her hand either.

As the moon appeared from behind a cloud, outlining the auberge, Libby breathed a sigh of relief. Home. She gently but resolutely removed her hand from Lucas's clasp. Her hand had felt far too comfortable resting in Lucas's capable one and she didn't want to give him any ideas.

Later after Lucas had left, she locked

up the auberge and secured the shutters against the gale that appeared to be getting up, before making her way upstairs to bed. Laying in bed listening to the wind howling through the trees, Libby thought about the evening and Lucas. She really liked him but she meant what she'd told Helen — she didn't need a man in her life. However gentle and attractive the man. For some reason, though, her last thought as she drifted into a fitful sleep while the wind whipped around the house was that Lucas and Dan would have been friends if they'd ever met.

15

Odette

'What time is your appointment with the immobilier?' Odette asked Isabelle as they walked along the canal path towards the auberge. Libby had invited them for lunch.

'Two thirty, so plenty of time,' Isabelle said. Debris from the storm still littered the path in places and she stopped to pick up a branch and throw it into the bank. 'This house sounds exactly what I'm looking for. In a small hamlet, three bedrooms, a good-sized kitchen, a large garden and neighbours not too close. Plus it's not too far away from you.'

'Good. I'm looking forward so much to having you living back up here,' Odette said. 'I've really missed not having you around. Besides, I'll be able to help you with . . . with things,' she added, looking at Isabelle.

Isabelle laughed and stood still to look at her mother. 'You've guessed, haven't you?'

Odette tried to look innocent but failed. 'Guessed what?'

'That I'm pregnant and you're going to be a grandmother.'

Odette smiled and hugged her daughter. 'I wasn't sure but hoped I was right. So exciting. When is it due?'

'Early February.'

'And Laurent? Is he thrilled?'

'Now that he's got used to the idea. The fact that I've decided to come back here has helped. We didn't plan this baby and he's been worried about how I'm going to cope with him being away so much.'

Odette hooked her arm through Isabelle's and they continued walking. 'Oh it'll be such fun having a baby in the family. Can we tell Libby today?'

Isabelle smiled. 'Of course.'

Libby was setting the table for lunch

under the loggia when they arrived. 'Is Bruno not with you?' she asked.

'He's joining us later,' Odette said. 'He sends his apologies but he had an appointment in Quimper. He said to go ahead and start lunch without him.'

'It's quiche and salad so not a problem to keep him some back,' Libby said, looking at Odette and Isabelle. 'You're both looking very happy with life today. Any special reason? Or just looking forward to your holiday?'

'I'm an expectant grandmother,' Odette told her excitedly, unable to keep the news to herself a moment longer. Both Isabelle and Libby laughed at the way she'd delivered the happy news.

'Wow. Congratulations both of you. I'd open a bottle of bubbly but I guess you're not drinking?' Libby said, looking at Isabelle. 'We'll save it to wet the baby's head instead.' Both Isabelle and Odette looked at her blankly. 'It's an English tradition for after the baby's born,' Libby explained.

'You pour champagne over the baby's head?' Odette asked.

Libby laughed. 'No. It's just what we call opening a bottle of wine, champagne or whatever, to toast the new arrival.'

'You have it with toast?' It was Isabelle's turn to sound incredulous.

'No!' Libby said, shaking her head. Some things definitely got lost in translation. 'When the baby is born I'll introduce you to the tradition. It'll be easier than trying to explain it now. Shall we eat?'

Sitting around the table eating and listening to her daughter and Libby chatting away, Odette felt content for the first time in months. Since selling the auberge to Libby and moving to the village, her life had seemed to lack any sort of real purpose, but everything was about to change again. There were things to look forward to now. Isabelle moving back to Brittany. A grandchild next year. A holiday in the south of France starting tomorrow. She reached down and picked up her bag.

'Libby, I forget to ask you. Would it be a problem for you to look after my houseplants while we are away? One visit in the middle of the week to water should be sufficient. I give you the key.' She put the spare house key on the table.

'No problem,' Libby said. 'Don't forget to send me a postcard or two, will you?

'I promise. Now Isabelle and I have to leave. We have a house to look at this afternoon.'

'Exciting,' Libby said. 'I'm looking forward to having you live near. Chloe will be pleased too.'

★ ★ ★

Odette didn't need telling that the house nestling in a nearby valley was an immediate *coup de foudre* for Isabelle the moment she set eyes on it. As the estate agent showed them around Odette could see Isabelle mentally painting and decorating rooms, especially the small one at the front of the house which would be an ideal nursery.

'I have to show another couple around later this afternoon,' the agent said quietly.

Isabelle glanced at him. 'I make an offer now and you tell the owner *immediament?*'

'Don't be pressured into anything,' Odette said, knowing how impulsive Isabelle could be. 'It's a lovely house but there will be others I'm sure. And won't Laurent want to see it before you decide?'

Isabelle shook her head. 'This one ticks all our — my — boxes.' She turned to the agent. 'Tell me the price again?' She nodded when she heard. 'OK. I'll give the full asking price on one condition. I want to sign this afternoon.'

16

Evie and Libby

Evie methodically went through her cooling-down stretching exercises after doing an hour's barre work. Thank goodness her ankle was back to its normal size now and she could move it without pain. It was getting stronger every day.

A quick shower and then she'd tidy up the sitting room. Libby was coming over for a coffee later and she wanted to make sure the gîte was presentable.

The chairs forming the makeshift barre in the corner needed to be put back in their proper place, and the wigs on the stand in the bedroom could go in the bottom of the wardrobe where they wouldn't be seen if for some reason Libby went into the bedroom. She also needed to get the rent ready to give to Libby.

She was in the kitchen setting up the coffee machine when Libby arrived. 'Hi, I made a raspberry clafoutis yesterday so I've bought a couple of slices,' Libby said. 'And before you say anything, it's fat-free. You can have a small piece and go for a walk this afternoon if you're worried about putting on weight. Can't see why you would be though. You're so slim.'

'Thanks. I'm not too bothered about my weight now that I'm mobile again and can exercise,' Evie said, taking a couple of plates out of the cupboard.

The sun was streaming in through the sitting-room windows as Evie placed the cakes and the coffees on the table and the two of them sat down.

'There's a small wrought-iron table and two chairs in the out-house,' Libby said. 'Would you like them for the terrace outside? Seems a shame you have nowhere to sit out there to enjoy the sunshine.'

'Thanks. Sounds good.'

'I'll pull them out later and give them

a bit of a clean-up,' Libby promised. 'I have to say, I love what you've done in here to personalise it. I'll have to pick your brains when I get time to start on my apartment. Right now it's just a place I sleep in.'

'I would love to help,' Evie said.

'These cushions are stunning,' Libby said, picking one up and examining the intricate beadwork. 'I guess you bought them in Paris?'

Evie shook her head. 'No. Well I bought the material there, but I made them myself. It's a hobby — helps to pass the time when . . . ' She stopped, realising she had been about to say 'when I'm backstage during rehearsals and performances'. Embarrassed, she jumped up and went into the bedroom. As comfortable as she felt with Libby, she didn't want anyone to know her secret yet.

'I make clothes as well. You like this jacket?' she asked, taking the white velvet jacket with its embroidered tribute to Lesage out of the wardrobe and turning to show it to Libby, who'd followed her and was standing in the doorway. Evie quickly pushed the wardrobe door closed. 'This is the latest jacket I've made.'

'That is so beautiful. You are very talented,' Libby said.

'Thanks. How are you enjoying life in France and being an auberge keeper?' Evie asked as they moved back into the sitting room. The conversation was in danger of becoming too personal for her liking. Any minute now Libby would be asking what she did for a living in Paris. A question she had no desire to answer. 'Is it like you dreamed it would be?'

Libby laughed. 'Not a bit. I'm far busier than I'd expected to be. I'd sort of thought, even when there were guests, the days would be my own to mooch around and enjoy the place. But keeping on top of everything — the laundry, the cleaning, the cooking, especially when all six bedrooms are occupied — is never-ending. Not to mention the chickens and the garden. And this week, with the excitement of the tree falling, it's been extra-hectic. I'm enjoying it though, and glad I took the plunge. Brittany is beautiful.'

'It is,' Evie agreed. 'But you must make time for yourself.'

'Sorry, did I sound as if it's all work and no time to play?' Libby said. 'It isn't really. I do have a social life as well. Next Saturday I'm going to the jazz festival with Lucas.'

'I also go out on that evening,' Evie said. 'So we both have the social life.'

'Going anywhere nice?'

'Just dinner with a new friend,' Evie replied. Picking up an envelope from the table, she handed it to Libby. 'The rent for the next month. Perhaps you check to make sure it's correct.'

'I'm sure it is. Oh — ' Libby looked at her. ' — you didn't have to go to the trouble of getting me cash. A cheque would have been fine.'

'It wasn't any trouble,' Evie said, shrugging. She couldn't tell Libby that

Evie Patem didn't have a bank account, and it was out of the question to have given her a cheque written by Suzette Shelby.

Libby left soon after and Evie took the empty cups and plates through to the kitchen. She'd wash them later. Right now she wanted to go for a walk and think about things. Her mobile rang as she picked up her camera.

'Hello, Malik. How are you?'

'Fine. How's the ankle? Doing your exercises?'

'Yes. I promised you I would.'

'Good. Any chance of you coming back here in the next few weeks? I need to talk to you.'

'No. I've just rented somewhere for a couple of months.'

'A couple of months?'

Evie could hear the panic in Malik's voice. 'Yes. I've told you several times I need some time on my own. You can talk to me now.'

'I've had an idea about your next career.'

Evie sighed. 'Tell me.'

'Next time I see you. I need to talk to a few people to see if it's feasible — no reason why it wouldn't be, but you know me. I like to cover all eventualities.'

Silently Evie substituted the word 'control' for 'cover'. Malik did like to feel in charge, even if in this case he wasn't. She was beginning to get her own ideas for a life after dance.

* * *

The Saturday of the jazz festival was a busy one for Libby. Four sets of guests moving out meant four bedrooms to be cleaned and aired, and beds made up for the next arrivals. Thankfully Agnes was willing to do more hours now the season was in full swing.

Libby had taken the decision as the summer became busier not to do meals on the evenings of change-over days — a decision she was thankful for by late afternoon when all the chores were finally finished and she could relax.

Not sure what the evening ahead would hold in the form of food, if anything, Libby made herself a ham-and-salad baguette and a pot of her favourite Earl Grey tea.

Chloe rang as she was finishing her food. 'Everything all right?' Libby asked. 'How did the ball go?'

'It was wonderful. Seems like a dream now. Mum, I've been thinking about your birthday. Would you mind if — '

'Please don't say you're not coming over,' Libby interrupted.

'Of course I'm coming. I wouldn't miss it for the world. I just want to know if it's OK for me to bring a friend.'

'You know it is.' Libby waited a second or two for Chloe to name her friend, but when she didn't speak Libby herself said, 'I'm off out to the jazz festival this evening so I need to shower and get ready.'

'Sounds fun. Who are you going with?'

'Lucas.' Libby said his name reluctantly, knowing that Chloe was likely to make a big deal of it.

To her surprise though, Chloe simply said, 'Enjoy. He's a nice man. Got to go. Love you, Mum. Bye.'

'Bye,' Libby echoed.

Once showered, Libby flicked through the hangers in her wardrobe wondering what to wear. In the end she settled for a favourite flower-patterned tea dress that had a hint of the 1930s about it and a scarlet pashmina to throw around her shoulders if the evening grew cold.

To Libby's delight Lucas was driving the Delage when he arrived. 'I am honoured,' she said, coming out of the auberge and locking the door behind her. 'I've been dying for a ride in your car.'

'*Bonsoir*,' Lucas said, kissing her on both cheeks before opening the passenger door for her.

Evie was sitting outside the gîte as they drove out onto the canal path. 'Enjoy your evening,' Libby called out as they passed.

Evie waved happily back at them. 'You too.'

'I'd forgotten she was going out this evening as well,' Libby said. 'I hope she has a good time. I don't think she's been very happy recently.'

'Why d'you say that?' Lucas asked.

Libby shrugged. 'Just a feeling I have.'

Libby was surprised at the amount of traffic making its way down to Chateauneuf. 'I didn't realise it was such a big festival,' she said.

'It's grown over the last few years,' Lucas said. 'Nothing like the music festival in Carhaix of course, but we do get some well-known jazz players turning up.'

After parking the car, Lucas took a picnic hamper out of the boot. 'I could have contributed something,' Libby said. 'You should have told me.'

Lucas shook his head. 'My treat. But if you can take one side of the basket it will be easier to carry. Right, let's join the party. Everyone should be over — ah, there they are.'

Carrying the hamper between them,

they made their the way over to a cluster of people laughing and joking together as they all arranged themselves on picnic rugs spread out on the bank of the river. As Lucas started making the introductions, a glass of rosé was thrust into Libby's hand.

Knowing there was no way she'd remember all their individual names — there must have been at least ten of them — Libby simply smiled at everyone as she said, '*Bonsoir.*' She'd get Lucas to whisper the names to her again, slowly, when they were settled on the rug themselves.

As food started to be passed around Libby noticed Lucas was drinking lemonade. 'Not drinking?' she asked.

'After ten o'clock this evening I'm on emergency call-out so I can't take the risk. We only get the occasional night call out, but . . . ' He shrugged. 'I have to be ready. I can eat, though, and these are delicious.' He picked up a small cocktail biscuit with a sliver of smoked salmon and some caviar perched on it and held it up to Libby's mouth. 'Try.'

Obediently, Libby opened her mouth and Lucas fed her. The seemingly innocent act turned into something more intimate as Lucas held her gaze for several seconds, smiling at her. In that instant Libby realised her feelings towards Lucas were changing. When he placed his arm around her shoulders as they settled down together on the rug, she didn't move away.

Lucas's friends included her in their conversations, although it was obvious they shared a lot of history and there were several in-jokes from past festival parties which, delivered in rapid French, Libby didn't always catch. But she didn't mind. She felt strangely content and happy just being there with Lucas.

Sitting watching as the swallows made their last swoops of the day over the river to scoop up a final supper of insects, seeing the stars and the moon appear in the darkening sky and listening to a young French girl sing the classic Edith Piaf song 'Non, *Je Ne Regrette Rien*',

Libby knew the magic of the evening would stay in her memory for ever.

When at half past ten Lucas frowned and took his mobile phone out of his pocket, Libby sighed, knowing instinctively the evening was about to end.

'I'm sorry, Libby. An old client has an emergency with her dog. I have to go. I'll ask Marc if he'll take you home.'

'Can't I come with you?' Libby asked. Staying on without Lucas didn't appeal. 'Or you could drop me off on your way?'

'Wrong direction. You sure about coming? Could be a long call.'

'I'm sure,' Libby said, jumping up and beginning to pack things away in the hamper.

* * *

As Lucas negotiated his way out of the crowded car park and drove up through the village, Libby asked, 'What kind of emergency is it?'

'A collie bitch giving birth. Its owner,

Eliane, is in her eighties and does tend to panic. When we get there everything will probably be proceeding as normal.' He shrugged. 'But I couldn't leave Eliane to worry.'

There was no mistaking Eliane's cottage when they reached the hamlet where she lived. It was the only cottage with lights on and the door open.

'Shall I come in with you?' Libby asked. 'Or would you prefer me to wait here?'

'Come in with me. I might need your help.'

Lucas opened the boot of the Delage and took out a large Gladstone-type bag and another smaller one.

'My emergency kits. I haven't got a full range in here, just the basic stuff. Here's hoping the dog doesn't need a caesarean.'

Lucas called out to Eliane as they walked into her cottage. She was sitting in a low chair quietly talking to Meg, her collie dog, who was lying on lots of newspapers on top of a folded blanket panting and straining hard. Three tiny black shapes lay alongside her.

Lucas dropped to his knees and gently examined the dog. 'Everything looks and feels normal,' he said, looking up at Eliane and smiling. 'How long has Tess been in labour?'

'Four hours,' Eliane said. 'The last pup came about half an hour ago.'

'*Bon*. The final one is on its way now.'

Libby held her breath as she saw the tiny black-and-white face of the pup push its way out into the world. A female, it was the smallest of the litter and Libby watched, fascinated, as Meg licked and cleaned it.

'She's beautiful,' she whispered.

Once Lucas was satisfied everything was as it should be and they'd helped Eliane clear the messy residue of newspapers away, they said good night and left.

'It was as I thought,' Lucas said. 'Eliane panicking. I am *desolé* our evening was spoiled by a non-emergency.'

'I wouldn't have missed it for

anything. I've never seen a puppy born before,' Libby said as they strapped themselves into the car. 'I wanted to smuggle that little female one away with me.' She glanced at Lucas. 'What d'you think Eliane will do with the puppies? She won't keep them, will she?'

'She's probably got a couple of local farmers ready to take them, especially if the father is a working collie.' Lucas slipped the car into gear. 'Right. Let's get you home.'

The roads were deserted and it seemed to Libby mere minutes before they were pulling up in front of the auberge and the evening was all but over.

'Would you like to come in for a nightcap or a mug of hot chocolate in case you get another call out?' she asked, getting out of the car.

'Thank you. Hot chocolate rather than a nightcap would be great,' Lucas said.

Standing companionably in the kitchen waiting for the milk to warm, Libby said, 'Thank you for this evening. I really enjoyed it.'

'*Bon*. So did I,' Lucas said. 'Next time I take you for dinner to my favourite restaurant.'

Libby smiled. 'Sounds good to me.' So they were going to see each other again, were they?

Stirring hot chocolate granules into the warm milk, she paused as car lights flashed past the kitchen window. 'Evie's home,' she said. 'I hope she's enjoyed her evening too.'

Lucas glanced out at the car now parked outside the gîte. 'That's Pascal's car,' he said, surprised. 'She's spent the evening with Pascal?'

Libby shrugged. 'I don't know. But why are you so surprised if she did?'

'His mother is *très* demanding. She's a nice lady but she leans on Pascal a lot, especially since her husband died. He's had to put his own life on hold.'

Libby gave the mugs a final stir before handing one to Lucas. 'I hope it's hot enough.'

'*Merci*.' To Libby's surprise, instead of taking a sip, Lucas put the mug down on the work surface before taking her by the hand, pulling her gently towards him and giving her a tender kiss.

★ ★ ★

Having waved goodbye to Libby and Lucas as they left for the evening, Evie sighed as they disappeared from view. Picking up her wine glass with the small amount of rosé she'd poured, she took a sip. Normally she didn't drink when she was alone, but tonight she'd felt in need of something to relax her and hopefully lift her spirits.

A big part of her was panicking at the thought of the evening ahead. For so long her social life had been wrapped up with her fellow dancers. People she knew. People she had a connection with.

It was years since she'd been out to dinner with a man on her own, other than Malik of course. What did she and her dinner date have in common? Why had he invited her? What would they find to talk about? She knew nothing about his world, and he thought she was somebody else entirely.

Evie gave a quick glance at her watch. It would be too cruel to cancel at this late hour, so she'd better go and get ready. Not knowing where she was likely to be taken gave her a major problem about what to wear. In the end she settled for a just-above-the-knees pink-and-grey button-through dress with a bolero jacket she'd customised with some delicate silver embroidery around the cuffs and hem. Smart and dressy enough for a hotel dining room but not too flashy for somewhere more down-market. She did feel good, though, making a proper effort to dress up after the weeks of dressing casually.

She heard the car stop outside the gîte and the door slam as she slipped her favourite pearl-stud earrings into her ears.

'*Bonsoir*, Pascal.'

'*Bonsoir. Ca va?*' Pascal asked as they kissed cheeks.

Evie nodded. 'Can I get you an aperitif or anything before we go?'

Pascal shook his head. '*Non, merci.* I've booked a table in Huelgoat. I hope that's all right? One of the lakeside restaurants. It will take us about thirty minutes to get there.'

'Sounds perfect,' Evie said. 'I've not been to Huelgoat yet.'

As the powerful car ate up the miles, conversation between them was limited as Pascal concentrated on his driving down the narrow twisting countryside lanes and Evie contented herself looking at the passing scenery. When Pascal pressed a button on the CD player and classical piano music began to fill the air, Evie smiled.

'I adore Chopin,' she said. 'Do you play the piano?'

'A little but I'm no expert. I just like to amuse myself these days. *Et vous?* You play?

Evie shook her head. '*Non.* Perhaps you play for me one day?'

'It would be my pleasure,' Pascal said.

Huelgoat Lake was as calm as the proverbial millpond as they drove into the village and made their way round to the restaurant. The terrace table they were shown to was secluded with an unobscured view of the lake. Perfume from honeysuckle and jasmine plants in large pottery urns placed at random points on the patio wafted around them.

'This is lovely,' Evie said after they'd given the waiter their starter and main course choices. 'D'you come here often?'

'First time,' Pascal said. 'I wanted somewhere new to both of us. It has a good reputation.'

'The postcard you sent me inviting me to dinner — was that the village school you went to?'

Pascal nodded. 'It had of course been modernised by the time I got there!'

'Is it still there?'

'For the moment. But numbers are going down every year when families move away to find work.'

'You've never had any ambition to

move away?' Evie said.

'Once, yes. After three years at university in Paris I had plans to travel the world. Instead it was straight back here to help with the estate,' Pascal said. 'My father was ill so I didn't have much choice.' He swirled some wine around his glass. 'When he died my mother needed me, so I've never left.'

'Any regrets?' Evie asked quietly.

Pascal smiled and shrugged. 'One or two. But on the whole I'm happy enough with my life these days. Besides, it doesn't do to look back too often. And who knows what's around the corner. Who you might meet.' He looked at her and held her gaze for several seconds before saying, 'Enough about me. Your turn to tell me how your life has been so far.'

To Evie's relief the waiter arrived at that moment with their starters and she was able to leave the question unanswered. What could she truthfully say to Pascal without revealing who she was? She knew instinctively he would dislike being lied to; their friendship would be over before it had barely begun. And sitting there as dusk began to fall, she realised she would enjoy getting to know this quiet, kind man better.

Candle torches were lit on the terrace and the waiter added a couple of small candles in the centre of their table. As they waited for their desserts Pascal admired the embroidery on her jacket. He gently fingered the silver thread-work of leaves and tiny beads around the cuffs of the jacket. 'This is so delicate and beautiful,' he said.

'Thank you,' Evie said. 'It's a hobby of mine. More of a passion really,' she laughed. 'There's a Fête des Brodeuses soon down in Pont-l'Abbé. I'm trying to work out how I can visit as I don't have a car.'

'I'll take you,' Pascal offered immediately.

'Oh no. I didn't mean that. I couldn't . . . '

'I will take you,' Pascal said. 'It is decided.'

'Truly? What about the garden centre?'

Pascal smiled at her. 'I am allowed the occasional day off you know. The place will survive without me for twenty-four hours.'

'In that case, thank you,' Evie said. 'And lunch will be on me that day.'

'We'll see,' Pascal said.

In the car driving home Pascal glanced at Evie before asking, 'You never did tell me how your life's been so far. Whether you too have any regrets?'

Evie was quiet. She'd been hoping that Pascal had forgotten about the unanswered question. As the silence lengthened between them, Pascal leant forward and pressed the CD button. This time the music that poured into the car was from Tchaikovsky's *Nutcracker Suite*. A piece of music that Evie could, if she'd played an instrument, have picked out note by note, she was so familiar with it.

She smothered a sigh before saying, 'Life has been mainly in Paris for the last oh, thirty years. And now . . . Now

I'm at a bit of a crossroads. Lots of decisions to be made.' She looked across at him. 'I will tell you my life history one day if you're interested, I promise. Just not tonight.'

'And I promise you I am interested and shall definitely hold you to that promise,' Pascal said.

Evie's heart lurched at his words and the quick, intense look her gave her. Pascal's shy diffidence, she was beginning to realise, hid an enviable inner strength.

17

Libby and Evie

The next morning Libby was on autopilot as she prepared and served breakfasts to her guests. When they'd all finished and left for the day she stacked the dishwasher and switched the coffee machine on again before making her way over to the gîte. The rest of her chores could wait for an hour.

Evie was rapidly becoming the closest thing she had to a girl friend and she was desperately in need of talking to somebody about the events of last night. And, if she was honest, she also wanted to hear how Evie's evening with Pascal had gone.

Evie called out, '*Attendez s'il vous plaît*, two minutes,' in response to Libby's knock.

When she did partially open the

door, Libby sensed she'd interrupted something. She'd never seen Evie so dishevelled before — wrinkled leggings, baggy T-shirt, and her hair all over the place.

'I'm sorry to barge in. Just wanted to say the coffee's on if you'd like one. But if you're busy . . . '

'I just exercise my ankle,' Evie said. 'I shower and come over, *oui?*' The door closed before Libby's 'OK' had left her lips.

Thoughtfully, Libby checked on the chickens before she went back indoors. Evie was definitely not herself this morning. Had something happened with Pascal last night?

But when Evie walked into the auberge kitchen ten minutes later she was her normal charming self. Fitted black jeans and a scooped neck white top had replaced her earlier outfit and her hair was combed into its usual immaculate style.

Libby did a double take at her hair. Surely Evie was wearing a wig? She'd never noticed before. Absently she poured the coffee.

'Did you enjoy the jazz last night?' Evie asked.

'It was great. Lucas had an emergency call-out that turned out not to be an emergency, and that was great too,' Libby said, trying to ignore the suspicion that was suddenly running through in her mind. 'And you? Your dinner date?' she asked as she mentally began to add up all the things she knew about Evie. Injured ankle. Lived in Paris. Said she'd been ill recently. Watched her weight ferociously. Wore a wig — was that a disguise? Had never really talked openly about her life.

Evie smiled. 'I had a nice time. Libby, why are you looking at me like that?'

Libby took a deep breath before saying, 'You'll probably think me mad. But I have to ask you anyway. Are you by any chance Suzette Shelby the famous missing ballerina?'

★　★　★

The words 'Are you by any chance Suzette Shelby the famous missing ballerina?' hung unanswered in the air between Libby and Evie for a full minute as Evie struggled with her conscience.

She did so want to continue being anonymous for the rest of the summer. She liked being an ordinary person, living a simple existence in the country. Being accepted as a friend without any ulterior motives or thoughts. Once people knew who she was their attitude towards her was sure to change.

But would her growing friendship with Libby be damaged beyond repair if she laughed and said, 'Gosh, no of course I'm not. Whatever gave you that idea?' Libby would only have to Google her and inevitably the truth would come out. Libby could then accuse her of lying, with some justification.

Silently Evie picked up the coffee Libby had poured for her and took a sip. 'Shall we sit down?' she said. Not waiting for an answer, she pulled out a kitchen chair and sat at the table. Libby sat opposite her and waited.

'Why d'you think I'm Suzette Shelby?' Evie said. Were other people also going to start jumping to the same conclusion?

'Just a feeling I got this morning,' Libby said, shrugging. 'The few things I know about you all suddenly came together when I realised you were wearing a wig. Injured ankle, you live mostly in Paris, you watch your weight when you're already slimmer than the average woman ... ' Libby paused. 'And then there's the way you move and avoid talking about yourself.'

Evie smiled ruefully. So not mentioning anything about her life in Paris had been seen as suspicious, making people wonder about her. Time to own up, with Libby at least.

'You're right. I am Suzette Shelby,' she said quietly.

'You are? Truly?' Libby said. 'You know, if you'd denied it I'd have believed you,' Libby said. 'Believed I'd made a mistake.'

'I didn't want to lie to you, Libby,' Evie said.

'Haven't you already by saying you're someone you're not?'

Evie shook her head. 'I don't think so. All those things you've just pointed out about me are true. And I've deliberately tried not to talk about my life to you precisely because I don't like lying.'

'Calling yourself by a different name isn't lying?' Libby asked.

'Evie Patem isn't a total lie. Evie is short for Evelyn, which is my middle name, and Patem was my grandmother's maiden name. So, a half lie?'

'Oh Evie,' Libby said. 'Or do I call you Suzette now?'

'Can we stay with Evie please?' Evie said, hesitating before adding, 'I'd really appreciate you keeping my secret.'

'It's not my secret to tell, nor is it any of my business what you call yourself,' Libby said. 'So I promise not to tell. But can I ask you why? Why bury yourself here in rural Brittany under an assumed name?'

'Because I needed space and time alone to think where there was nobody — like Malik my ex-partner — to apply pressure: keep exercising, keep dieting, keep in the spotlight.' She drained her coffee mug. 'I know my career as a ballerina will finish this autumn and I needed to decide what to do next. I didn't think I could exist away from the world of dance but living here, alone, is showing me I can.' She smiled at Libby. 'I'm finally beginning to realise I still have a lot of life to live.'

'So at the end of summer you'll leave, go back to Paris and become Suzette Shelby again,' Libby said. 'The retired ballerina.'

Evie fiddled with her coffee cup, thinking about Libby's words. That was of course Plan A. Though she'd never truly realised, until Libby said the words, that 'retired ballerina' was exactly how she would be viewed in the future. The phrase made her feel so old.

'Yes. When I leave here, Evie Patem

will be relegated to the past. A fond memory and a secret between you and me.' She smiled at Libby.

'Anytime Suzette feels the need to get away, Evie will always be welcome to visit,' Libby said, smiling back at her. 'And now tell me, where did Pascal take you last night?'

'How did you know it was Pascal?' Evie asked, surprised.

'Lucas recognised his car.' Libby hesitated before adding, 'He was surprised, to be honest. He said Pascal's mother has a huge influence on his life. Controlling even.'

Evie nodded. 'He explained to me last night about his father dying and his mother needing him.'

'So where did he take you last night?'

'A lakeside restaurant in Huelgoat,' Evie said. 'We had a lovely meal. He's such a . . . ' She hesitated before adding quietly, ' . . . gentleman.' The word described Pascal perfectly.

'D'you think you'll see him again?' Libby asked.

'He's promised to take me to the Pont-l'Abbé Embroidery Festival,' Evie said. 'So he does manage to get away from his mother from time to time. I think maybe my fellow countrymen are used to handling the most domineering of mothers!'

18

Libby

Libby was busy tidying the auberge sitting room when Helen rang Friday morning. 'We need to talk about your birthday party,' she said without any preamble. 'It's not long now.'

'It's weeks away,' Libby protested.

'And time flies when you're not ready,' Helen continued. 'Now, do you need me to bring anything for the party you can't get over there?'

'I'm not sure you'd call the nibbles and champagne I'm planning a party.'

'Libby, people expect more from you. Champagne of course, but nibbles? You have to mark the occasion with a proper party. Have you made a list of people you want to come?'

Libby sighed. Helen was clearly in no mood to listen. 'I don't need to write a list. It will just be you and Peter, Odette and Bruno, Isabelle, Lucas, Evie, Chloe and her friend. That's about it. Talking of Chloe, how is she?'

'She's fine. Told me the other night she's really looking forward to coming over.'

'Who's the friend she's bringing?' Libby asked casually. 'Presumably they'll travel over with you?'

'I think they intend making their own way. I've booked the ferry tickets for the day before so I can give you a hand getting ready. Now you're sure there's nothing you want me to bring?'

'Can't think of a single thing,' Libby said. 'No, wait — there is one thing I can't find over here, and that's large bags of peanuts for the birds. If you could bring a few with you that would be great.'

Helen gave a loud exasperated sigh. 'Libby, you're impossible. I'll talk to you later.'

It was only after she'd put the phone down that Libby realised Helen hadn't answered her question about who Chloe was bringing with her.

Libby glanced at her watch. 11:30. Just about time to walk along the canal path to the village shop before they closed for lunch. She took Odette's house keys from the hook. She'd check on her houseplants at the same time.

As she set out a group of cyclists were making their way leisurely along the canal path, carefully avoiding the worst of the pot-holes and the tree roots that were pushing up through the tarmac in places. By the time Libby had reached and was climbing the steps up to the lane that linked the path to the village, she'd said *bonjour* to a number of walkers who were out enjoying the sunshine and the peaceful countryside.

Quickly buying the baguettes and milk she needed from the shop, she walked on down through the village to Odette's mas. As she pushed open the wrought-iron gates that separated the house from the road, Lucas pulled up alongside her.

'*Bonjour. Ca va?*' he asked, winding down his car window.

'I'm fine. You?' Libby said, smiling.

That was the thing with Lucas; seeing him invariably made her smile.

'I was on my way to see you,' he said. 'My sister Veronique is here and I wondered if you'd like to come to lunch tomorrow? I'd say supper but I guess you have visitors to feed then?'

'I'd love lunch tomorrow,' Libby said. 'Thank you. Can I bring anything?'

Lucas shook his head. 'Just yourself. About twelve o'clock. Have to go; I'm running late.'

Wandering around Odette's house watering her various plants, Libby realised she'd completely forgotten that tomorrow was change-over day, generally her busiest day of the week. Thankfully Agnes was booked to work tomorrow from 8 a.m. and there were only four bedrooms to change and clean. And even better, none of the new guests were due to arrive before five o'clock, so plenty of time to get back from Lucas's.

Watering the last plant on the windowsill in the sitting room, Libby briefly wondered what Veronique would be like.

★   ★   ★

The next morning, despite Lucas telling her she didn't have to bring anything, Libby didn't feel comfortable going empty-handed, so she filled a container with her homemade cheese biscuits to take with her. Leaving Agnes to help herself to lunch and promising to be back by three o'clock, she set off for her rendezvous at Lucas's. It was the first time she'd been to the Vetinaire Centre a kilometre or so outside the village, and she looked around as she parked alongside Lucas's muddy estate car.

A hedge of beech trees separated the modern single-storey building from the surrounding fields on three sides, while the front was open-plan with plenty of parking. Flowerbeds either side of the entrance were filled with sunflowers and daisies. As she got out of the car, the green flashing neon light on the building indicating the surgery was open stopped, the door opened and Lucas appeared.

238

'Welcome,' he said, kissing her on the cheeks three times. 'Come and meet Veronique.' Holding Libby by the hand, he led her through a maze of small rooms and into his apartment at the back of the building. 'Veronique has set everything up outside,' he said. 'I have to warn you, she can be a bit bossy sometimes,' he whispered. 'Comes over all big sisterish.'

Libby laughed. She couldn't imagine anyone bossing Lucas around.

French doors led from the kitchen onto a paved terrace, where Veronique was putting the finishing touches to the table for lunch. Lucas quickly made the introductions.

Libby found herself shaking hands with a tiny woman sporting a blonde elfin haircut. '*Bonjour*. Lovely to meet you,' she said. 'How long are you here for?'

'Just the weekend. I come up every couple of months to help Lucas sort out his paperwork. I'm an accountant and Lucas is useless with figures,'

Veronique added, shaking her head at her brother. 'Let's eat.' She gestured at the table. 'I'll fetch the first course.'

'I brought some homemade cheese biscuits,' Libby said. 'Lucas said I didn't need to bring anything, but . . . ' Libby shrugged apologetically as she offered the container to Veronique.

'He was right, but *merci,*' Veronique said before she bustled away to the kitchen.

'See, I told you she was bossy,' Lucas murmured.

'Bossy but nice,' Libby whispered back.

Conversation over lunch strayed from subject to subject, but for Libby the best part was when Lucas and Veronique began talking about their childhood. Lucas, according to his sister, had apparently been a very mischievous little boy, forever getting into scrapes that she had to rescue him from.

'No, no. That's not how I remember it at all,' Lucas said at one point, wagging his finger at Veronique. 'You were desperate to join in, not to rescue me.' He stopped as his mobile phone rang.

Veronique pulled a face at Libby and leant in to say quietly, 'Forever on call. Hope you can accept that.'

Surprised at her words, Libby looked at her, but before she could respond Lucas was on his feet. 'Sorry, girls. Accident on the route nationale. A cattle truck has got caught up in it. I have to go.' He turned to Libby. 'I'll ring you later. Don't dash off. Stay and talk to Veronique.' And he was gone.

Veronique sighed. 'I've lost count of the number of times emergency calls have interrupted Lucas's off-duty life.'

'It's like doctors, isn't?' Libby said thoughtfully. 'Neither profession is ever really off duty. But Lucas clearly loves what he does.'

19

Evie

Evie looked around her as Pascal drove them through the green undulating countryside and on down towards the coast, Pont-l'Abbé and the embroidery festival. 'I'm looking forward so much to today,' she said. 'Although I do feel guilty about taking you away from your work at the garden centre.'

'Don't,' Pascal said as he slowed down approaching a crossroads and the left turn that would take them into Pont-l'Abbé. 'We are going to have a fun day together. Forget all our work problems.'

Evie glanced across at him. He had problems with work too? 'But it's your business. You are in charge.'

Pascal nodded. '*Oui*. But always there are problems. With staff. With bureaucracy. With cash flow. With . . . ' He hesitated. 'Oh, just decisions to be made all the time.' He smiled at her. 'But today we forget all our problems and enjoy ourselves.'

The sound of Breton bagpipes, the smell of crêpes, processions, Breton dancing, doll exhibitions, costume exhibitions . . . The day passed in a whirl for Evie. She made note after note, collected business cards and brochures, took photos of some particularly intricate embroidery, and was totally amazed by everything she saw.

At one particular haute couture exhibition full of modern designer clothes, Pascal turned to her. 'Your embroidery is as good, no?' He stopped. 'It's better than anything on show here today, Evie. But I suspect you know that already.' He smiled at her. 'Is it what you intend doing in the future? Is that why you're making all these notes? Gathering information?'

'Perhaps,' Evie said, moving away to look at an intricate wedding dress. She wasn't ready to talk to Pascal yet about her idea.

'If you've got the inclination you can compete with the best of them and make a living.'

Something about the way he said the word 'inclination' and the phrase 'make a living' made Evie turn to look at him.

'You could do it anywhere too — you wouldn't have to live in Paris. You could live anywhere,' Pascal continued.

Evie inclined her head. 'Thank you. I know my embroidery is good. But moving out of Paris is another thing entirely. One that's definitely not on my current agenda.'

Pascal opened his mouth as if to say something, changed his mind and shrugged. 'Come on. Let's find somewhere to have a coffee before we head for home.'

'Thank you for today,' Evie said when they'd finally found a café with a spare table and the waitress had placed a cafetiere of coffee in front of them. 'I've really enjoyed it.' She hesitated and fiddled with a sugar packet before adding, 'I didn't mean to be rude

244

earlier, but I'm still trying to sort things out in my own mind.'

'I know. You said. You're at a crossroads.' Pascal placed his hand over Evie's twitching fingers and looked at her, a serious expression on his face. 'I've very much enjoyed today too. When you want to talk I'm ready to listen.'

'Thank you,' Evie said.

It wasn't until they were in the car halfway home that Pascal dropped what amounted to a bombshell to Evie. 'I have a confession to make. My mother wants to meet you and I half-promised I'd take you to see her before returning you to the gîte.' He glanced at her. 'I know it's been a long day and you're probably tired, but I'd really like the two of you to meet. You'll be disappearing back to Paris before we know it.'

Evie was silent for minute, remembering the word Libby had used about Pascal's mother. Controlling. She'd also heard her described as always being elegant and immaculately dressed.

Whereas she, Evie, at this moment was tired and her clothes after the day at the festival were no longer immaculate.

But she did owe Pascal something for taking her to Pont-l'Abbé. No, owe was the wrong word; she was truly grateful to Pascal and didn't want to hurt him by refusing to meet his mother.

'I'll understand if you're too tired,' Pascal said into the silence. 'We can make it another time.'

'No, this evening is fine,' Evie said. 'So long as your mother doesn't mind my creased clothes.' She glanced down at her cotton frock. Freshly ironed that morning, it was less than pristine now.

'Thank you. We won't stay long, I promise,' Pascal said.

Twenty minutes later Pascal turned into a tree-lined avenue and Evie saw the longhouse standing at the end of the drive for the first time. An involuntary gasp escaped from her lips. 'What a beautiful house,' she said.

'Tell my mother that and she'll love you forever,' Pascal said. 'She and my father spent years renovating it. It was practically derelict when they inherited it.'

As they got out of the car Evie saw Madame de Guesclin, poised and immaculate, standing in the doorway waiting to greet them.

After Pascal had introduced them, his mother led them through to the sitting room before turning to Pascal. 'You naughty boy. You left your phone behind. I haven't been able to contact you all day.'

'*Desolé*, Mama,' Pascal replied. 'Did you need me urgently?'

'No. I just wanted to know if you were having a good time. And . . . ' She paused. ' . . . whether you had learnt anything?'

'*Oui*. I learnt a lot about design and embroidery today.'

Evie looked at the two of them. She knew somehow that his answer was not what Madame de Guesclin had wanted to hear. There was an undercurrent here she didn't understand.

'Mademoiselle, may I offer you a small aperitif?' Madame de Guesclin gestured towards a decorative wooden side table, where on a highly polished silver tray several decanters of spirits and crystal glasses stood.

'A glass of apple juice would be nice,' Evie replied, seeing a bottle hidden in amongst the others. 'I don't drink spirits.'

As Pascal poured the drinks — apple juice for her, martini for his mother and pastis for himself — Evie became uncomfortably aware that she was being scrutinised. Surely her dress wasn't that creased?

'You like it here?' Madame de Guesclin said suddenly.

Evie nodded. 'I like it here very much. Of course I miss some things about Paris — the shops and the theatre mainly, but they'll still be there when I return.'

'Ah, I too adore the theatre,' Madame de Guesclin said. 'My husband used to take me regularly.' She sighed before asking abruptly, 'You find it quiet here after Paris?'

'*Oui*, but it is a wonderful tranquility,' Evie said. She finished her drink and placed the empty glass on the table. 'It has been a pleasure meeting you, Madame de Guesclin. Thank you for the aperitif, but now I'm afraid I'm going to have to ask Pascal to be my chauffeur again and take me home. It's been a long day.'

'Such a short visit. We've barely got to know one another. Maybe you come for dinner one evening before you disappear back to Paris?'

'Thank you.'

'I'll tell Pascal which evening will be convenient for me. *Bonsoir.*'

20

Odette

Odette fanned herself with the *Nice-Matin* newspaper she'd bought that morning as they'd passed the news-agent's kiosk on their way to the station to catch the train.

Impossible to believe they'd been down here for five days already. Five days of whirlwind sightseeing as Isabelle tried to show them all the places she'd come to know after three years of living down here. They'd explored Nice and strolled along the famous Promenade des Anglais. They'd gone along the coast to Antibes Juan-les-Pins and Cannes and today it was Monaco/Monte Carlo as the arrivals board at the station had announced it.

Ten o'clock and already the temperature in the principality was in the high twenties. It was a relief to sit at one of the tables outside the Café de Paris and order cold drinks. Whilst they waited, Bruno wandered over to look at two luxury red sports cars parked in front of the casino steps.

Isabelle, noticing a friend on another table, apologised to Odette and went over to have a quick chat with her before their drinks arrived.

Left to herself, Odette amused herself by people-watching for a few moments before unfolding her newspaper, scanning the headlines, and then flicking through the pages in search of something more interesting. A short feature at the bottom of the entertainment pages caught her eye.

'Where is Suzette Shelby? Mystery still surrounds the disappearance of the injured ballerina from her room in the Hotel de Paris, Monaco some weeks ago.' A small picture alongside the feature showed the ballerina dressed for her role in *Swan Lake* a couple of seasons previously.

Odette had never been a keen fan of ballet, but there was something about this photo that caught her attention. Something she couldn't quite put her finger on. How could a picture of somebody in costume for a ballet mean anything to her? She'd never met a ballet dancer in her life — aside of course from Madame Le Mairie in the village who a few years ago had given toddler Isabelle a few lessons in the village hall.

Even when she turned the page of the newspaper and went on to other features, she was drawn back to the picture. It definitely reminded her of something or somebody. But why?

Odette was still thinking about the picture when Isabelle returned. 'Are you OK?' Isabelle asked anxiously, looking at Odette. 'Do you need to put your sunglasses on? You're screwing your eyes up.'

'I'm fine,' Odette said. 'Just thinking about something. And I'm hot. Ah, our drinks. A cold lemonade will help.

Where are you taking us next?'

'I thought we'd have a quick look at the gaming rooms in the casino; they really are worth seeing,' Isabelle said. 'The chandeliers and the ornate decorations are amazing.'

'I think those cars come under that description too,' Bruno said, rejoining them and pulling a chair out. 'Although I think amazingly expensive would be a better description. Still, the engineering that goes into them . . . ' He shook his head.

'And after the casino?' Odette asked.

'We'll need to make our way up to the palace before midday to watch the changing of the guard,' Isabelle said. 'I thought afterwards you'd like to see the cathedral too; it'll be nice and cool in there. Then we'll lunch.'

'Sounds good,' Odette said. 'I can't believe we're nearly at the end of our holiday. All this sight-seeing has made the days go so quickly. But tomorrow we start the packing, yes?'

Isabelle smiled in agreement. 'Yes.

Then next week it's back to Brittany.'

'We've got a lot do before then,' Odette said.

It was only as they stood with the crowds in front of the palace later that morning to watch the changing of the guard that the truth behind the newspaper photograph dawned on her.

An involuntary '*Voilà!*' left her lips.

Isabelle turned to look at her.

'Sorry,' Odette muttered. 'I've just realised something.'

21

Evie

Evie, sitting outside the gîte enjoying the Sunday afternoon sunshine and trying to sketch an embroidery pattern for a bolero she intended to make for Libby, glanced up as a mud-spattered Land Rover drew up, Pascal at the wheel. She smiled in welcome as he jumped out, closely followed by a black-and-white dog who raced across to her.

'*Bonjour*,' Pascal said. 'Lola, behave.'

'She's adorable,' Evie said, stroking the dog. 'Tibetan Terrier?'

Pascal nodded. 'You like dogs?'

'Having one is high on my list as soon as . . . ' Evie paused before finishing, ' . . . as soon as it's possible.'

'I'm on my way to walk Lola. Care to join me?' Pascal asked.

Evie hesitated, briefly wondering

whether her ankle was up to a long, fast walk.

'Won't be a marathon, I promise,' Pascal said.

'In that case, I'd love to. I'll just put this away and change my shoes.'

'I have the dinner invitation my mother threatened you with,' Pascal said, reaching into his pocket and pulling out a large square envelope. 'I'm afraid she's old-fashioned and still insists on using these formal cards.'

Evie glanced at him as she took the invitation. 'Is it going to be a formal dinner too? How many invites has she issued?' Too many and she would send a regretful 'unable to accept your kind invitation'. As much as she liked Pascal, the idea of being scrutinised by his mother did not appeal.

'Two of her closest friends and their husbands. There will be about eight of us I expect; Mother can't abide odd numbers at the table. It will be fairly formal. You will come, though, won't you? Cook always does us proud.'

'You have a cook?' Evie said, surprised. Pascal's family was turning out to be even grander than she'd first thought.

'My mother is a terrible cook so my father insisted on employing one. Now he's gone I doubt that Mother would bother to eat if it wasn't for Marie,' Pascal said.

Thoughtfully, Evie placed the card on the table. Maybe there would be safety in numbers. Madame de Guesclin would surely limit herself to polite social conversation in front of her friends.

Five minutes later Pascal was driving the Land Rover in the direction of Gourin and heading for Tronjoly Park. Leaving the car and clipping Lola's lead on, they began to wander through the grounds surrounding the chateau. There were few other people about and strolling along the paths with Lola running ahead, her extension lead stretched to its limit, Evie began to remember long-ago walks in Parisian parks with her mother.

Solange Gady, disliking city life intensely, had taken every opportunity to escape either into the countryside surrounding Paris or even, when time allowed, out to Versailles where she would happily spend hours wandering around the grand chateau's grounds. A young Evie though, preferred their local park where she could feed the ducks and go on the swings. Teenage Evie, while enjoying the freedom from continual dance practice the train excursions gave her, knew it was her fault they had to live in Paris and she began to harbour feelings of guilt for making her mother live somewhere she hated.

'It won't be forever,' Solange had said repeatedly. 'Once you're an established star I shall move back to the country.'

Sadly that had never happened. Solange had lived long enough to see Evie become a principal dancer with a well-known ballet company; had even proudly travelled with her once or twice internationally. But when she'd finally decided it was time to release the reins and find her country cottage, fate stepped in and denied her the chance.

In the weeks before she died she talked to Evie in a way she never had before. Her sadness over the way she'd lived her life was almost the last thing she admitted. 'I know you adore dancing and are blessed with a rare gift, but promise me you'll one day try to live a different life. A normal one that involves people. Don't isolate yourself from people like I did. I don't want you to die with regrets like me.'

The phrase 'die with regrets' had haunted Evie ever since.

'You are quiet,' Pascal said. 'Perhaps we walk too far?'

'*Non*,' she hastened to reassure him. 'I was just remembering long-ago walks with my mother,' Evie added, suppressing a shiver at the memory of her mother's last words.

'It's really beautiful here. Oh look, there are ducks on the lake.'

Pascal looked at her thoughtfully. 'I think you are cold? We go for a coffee in Gourin.'

The centre of the town was quiet,

with a few tourists wandering around and inspecting the replica of the Statue of Liberty in the main street. Placed there as a reminder of the large number of emigrants from the area who had fled to America in the early part of the 20th century in search of a better life, its presence dominated that area of the town. For Evie it brought even more memories flooding back.

'Have you ever seen the original?' Evie said.

Pascal shook his head. '*Non*. You?'

'Several times, but the first time is the one I remember.'

Pascal glanced at her.

'My mother was with me. It was her first, and only, visit to New York too. Seeing the statue made her cry. It was the first time I ever saw her show emotion in public. For a French woman she kept everything under tight control. Never allowed anyone to see her true feelings.' Evie bit her lip as she remembered how unhappy she'd sensed her mother had been on that trip.

'Did she say why the statue affected her so much?'

Evie nodded. 'Her only brother was disowned by the family and emigrated when she was twelve. She never saw him again. He was killed in World War Two, leaving a widow and a year-old son.'

'So perhaps you have relatives in America?'

Evie nodded. 'I tried to persuade my mother to search for them while we were there but she wouldn't. She said she'd think about it for her next visit.' Evie raised a hand to her face to brush a tear away. 'Sadly, she never went again. She died two months after our visit. The Big C,' she added quietly in explanation.

Gently Pascal took her hand and squeezed it.

'I'm sorry. I don't know why I'm telling you all this,' Evie said. 'I rarely talk about it.'

'I'm glad you have. I would like to know everything about you in time,' Pascal said quietly. 'We get our coffee.'

Still holding her hand, he led her over to a nearby café and ordered their drinks.

'Your mother, she was born in Brittany?' Pascal asked as they waited for their coffees to arrive.

Evie nodded. 'A little hamlet about twelve kilometres away from here.'

'Is that why you came here after your accident?'

Evie recoiled. Did Pascal know who she was? She hadn't told him about her accident.

Sensing her anxiety, Pascal held her gaze. 'Agnes told me when you arrived at the gîte — you said you'd been ill and were recovering from a slight accident.'

Evie smiled. She should have remembered how notorious small villages were for knowing everybody's business. 'I suppose it's part of the reason. I do have vague memories of a holiday here once when I was about, oh, nine or ten I suppose. Mainly, though, it was because I wanted to go somewhere as different to Paris as possible.'

The young lad doing the waiting arrived with their coffees, carefully placing them on the table with an audible sigh of relief at not having spilt a drop. Gravely, Pascal thanked him as Evie smiled.

'First-job nerves I think,' Pascal said. 'I remember suffering.'

'I still do,' Evie said quietly, remembering the many first-night nerves she'd suffered during her career. Not wanting to explain further as she saw Pascal's quizzical look, she deliberately changed the conversation. 'Business is good at the garden centre now the weather is warming up?'

Pascal smiled at her before saying, '*Oui*. Business is brisk. And you? Have you thought any more about living somewhere other than Paris?'

Evie shook her head. '*Non*. I have a few more weeks before I have to make the decision. *Peut-être* by then I will have the answer.'

It was an hour later before Pascal dropped Evie back at the gîte. As she opened the passenger door he said, 'My mother's dinner invitation — you haven't said yes yet.'

Evie gave Lola a pat on the head before saying, 'Give me two minutes and I'll give you my formal reply.' She slipped out of the Land Rover and went into the gîte. Quickly she found a suitable piece of paper, wrote her reply, folded the paper and put it in an envelope. Back outside she found Pascal leaning against the Land Rover and handed the envelope to him.

'It's probably not formal enough for your mother but I'm afraid it's the best I can do,' she said.

'So, are you coming to dinner or not?'

'You'll have to ask your mother,' Evie teased. When she saw the look on Pascal's face she impulsively leant forward and kissed his cheek. 'Thank you for this afternoon. I've had a lovely time with you and Lola, who is adorable. And yes, I've accepted your mother's invitation.' Though heaven only knew what kind of evening she was letting herself in for.

22

Libby / Evie

'So what d'you reckon?' Libby asked Evie. She'd just given Evie the guided tour of her small apartment at the top of the auberge, hoping that she would be able to give her some inspiration for decorating the sitting room in a few weeks' time.

'It doesn't work at the moment, does it?' she asked now, looking around.

'I don't think it needs redecorating,' Evie said slowly. 'The walls are a good neutral colour. Maybe a cream throw over the settee would make a difference. It's quite a dominant feature in the room. Perhaps even change it for an old-fashioned daybed you can pile with cushions. Place it against the wall and leave the centre of the room free.'

Libby clapped her hands in delight.

'Evie, you're brilliant. It's my English furniture that's all wrong, isn't it? I need some French stuff up here.'

'An antique ormolu mirror on that wall would look good too,' Evie said. 'Gold decoration always adds something to a room.'

Libby looked around thoughtfully. 'I need to think . . . Oh, what's the phrase? Shabby chic. That's what I'll aim for. Shabby chic. Pale colours, distressed wood and an ornate mirror.'

'I have some cream velvet material I can make up into cushion covers for you,' Evie offered. 'I saw a couple of tapestry designs at the festival that I'd like to try and copy.'

'Thank you. I meant to ask you, how did your day with Pascal go?'

'It was great fun. I like Pascal a lot,' Evie said. 'And the festival was amazing. I got so many ideas. And . . . ' She hesitated before adding, ' . . . it confirmed that something I've been thinking about could be possible.'

Libby looked at her and waited.

'Could I bounce some ideas off you? I think discussing things would help me to decide what to do. And now you know my secret — ' Evie smiled. ' — I can talk to you.'

'Of course,' Libby said. 'Start bouncing!'

'Let's go down to the gîte and I can show you everything I've worked out so far.'

'Okay,' Libby said. 'Give me five minutes while I check on the guests in room two. They said they were staying in for the evening. I'd like to make sure they have everything they need.'

★　★　★

While she waited for Libby to join her, Evie placed the large file with her ideas, brochures and contact addresses on the small outside table and sat down ready to go through them again.

Should she stick to Plan A? Go back to Paris, dance a final ballet and then retire gracefully to her apartment and concentrate on her embroidery? Or was the Plan B that had been forming in her mind for hours now at all feasible? Hopefully talking it all over with Libby would help clear her mind; highlight the pros and cons of both plans.

Libby when she arrived looked at all the paperwork. 'You have been busy.' She picked up a glossy brochure showing lots of highly decorated haute couture dresses. Reading the accompanying price list, she glanced at Evie.

'Do people actually pay these prices?'

Evie nodded. 'Yes.'

'So, what d'you want to talk about?' Libby asked.

'I know my embroidery is as good as anything I've seen,' Evie said. 'So I'm convinced I can make a business out of it. The big question is, where do I set up business? Paris, or somewhere down here?'

'Why d'you want to stay in Brittany anyway?' Libby asked. 'I mean I love it here, but you've lived in Paris for so long. Surely you'd miss the hustle and bustle of the place?'

Evie shrugged. 'I've discovered I like it here. My family originated from here years ago so maybe it's in my genes.' She frowned as she searched through the file. 'I thought I had some sample materials in here. They seem to have disappeared. Oh, maybe I dropped them in Pascal's car. I'll ring him tomorrow and check.'

She sighed, picked up some loose papers and replaced them in the folder. 'I feel a bit guilty actually. Pascal told me I could do this from anywhere but I snapped his head off. I told him moving to Brittany wasn't a part of the plans for my future. Only since then I've been thinking. Why shouldn't it be? Rather than go back and become Suzette Shelby the retired ballerina who is now a needlewoman, why don't I stay here to do it? Continue to live as Evie Patem?'

Libby looked at her, dismay written all over her face. 'Oh Evie, you can't be serious. Just think about the problems it would create for you. Not with your work — although I think the name Suzette Shelby would open doors that might remain closed to an unknown Evie Patem — but with your personal life. Things like finding somewhere to live, registering with the doctor, opening a bank account. They'd all have to be done in your real name, so certain people would know who you were. Your name would be almost certain to leak out. Oh!' she stopped. 'I've just realised why you paid me in cash! And what if you meet someone special? I take it you haven't told Pascal your real name?'

Evie was silent for a moment. 'No. I like Pascal a lot but so far there's been no reason to tell him. We're just friends. And if I do decide to go back to Paris . . . ' She shrugged. 'Well, that will probably be the end of things anyway. Long-distance friendships rarely survive. And Pascal has said he hates going to cities.'

'Well if you do decide to live in Brittany, why not come clean and just tell everyone who you are?' Libby said.

'I'm not sure about doing that,' Evie said. 'Particularly as far as Pascal is concerned. Once the news leaked out the media would be swarming all over the place for days until they tire of the story. He'd hate the attention that invariably surrounds me.'

'I'm sure he'd cope,' Libby said.

They both turned to look at the canal as the sound of a boat's engine chugging downstream reached them.

'Do you have to go and work the lock for them?' Evie asked curiously.

Libby shook her head. 'No, thank goodness. People have to do it for themselves these days. This barge looks like one of the charter ones from up Brest way; they usually have a skipper on board to tell everybody what to do.'

As they watched, a man leapt onto the quay and began the process of opening the lock.

'I've never actually seen a boat going through the lock before,' Evie said. 'You don't seem to get many on this stretch of canal.'

'It's because they blocked the canal to build the dam at Lac de Guerlédan. I think there are probably more on the stretch down to Nantes,' Libby said, turning back to Evie. 'Like I was saying, I'm sure Pascal . . . Evie, whatever is the matter? You like like you've seen a ghost.'

Evie didn't answer; couldn't answer. She merely stared at the man who was now striding towards them.

'Surprise, surprise, Suzette. I've come to visit with you for a few days,' Malik said, smiling at her.

23

Suzette

Suzette, staring in shock at Malik, barely registered Libby's whispered 'I'll leave you to talk to your friend' before she left to return to the auberge.

'Malik, what are you doing here? More to the point, how did you find me?' Suzette demanded as Malik air-kissed her cheeks. 'And why? I told you I needed time alone.' She glared and moved away from him.

'You don't sound very pleased to see me,' Malik said, fingering the folder of papers that was still on the table. Suzette quickly snatched it up before he could start looking through it.

'I'm not,' she said. '*Desolé*, but that's the truth. I'll just put this indoors.' When she returned Malik was standing looking at the auberge.

'I have to admit, you've found yourself a lovely hiding place,' he said as she rejoined him.

'You haven't answered my questions,' Suzette said. 'Why and how?'

'I was concerned for you,' he said. 'Worried that you were maybe having a breakdown.'

'I told you I needed time to think about the future. Do I look as though I'm having a breakdown?'

Malik shook his head. 'No. You look very well. You're going to have to lose that extra weight, though, before *Swan Lake*.'

Suzette shrugged. 'It's only a couple of kilos. It won't take long to shift. Okay — you were concerned about me; that's the 'why' question taken care of. Next, how did you find me?'

'It was easy in the end. Your concierge,' Malik said. 'Although to be fair he didn't actually tell me. He gave me the envelope with your forwarding address on it and asked me to post it. I think he thought I knew where you were anyway. So I decided to act as postman. It's on board the boat waiting for you to collect.'

At the mention of the boat, Suzette glanced down towards the canal. 'Someone down there seems to be trying to attract your attention.'

Malik turned and waved his hand in acknowledgement. 'That's the skipper. He's waiting for us to go on board. The crew have supper waiting for us. Shall we go?'

'I'm not hungry.'

Malik sighed. 'So sit and watch me eat. We need to talk. And you can tell me whether you playing at being a wannabe Greta Garbo 'I want to be alone' has had the desired effect, and helped you reach a decision about the future.' He held out his hand to Suzette. 'Come on.' Reluctantly Suzette took it. 'Besides, I have a suggestion for you to think about,' Malik said.

'You said before. Why are you being so mysterious about it? I wish you'd just tell me.'

'Soon, I promise,' Malik said.

He continued to hold her hand as they walked away from the gîte and down towards the canal. Pascal's car was driving along the path towards the auberge as Suzette and Malik neared the boat. Raising her free hand in acknowledgement, Suzette smiled at him and waited for him to draw up alongside them.

'Pascal, meet Malik, an old friend of mine from Paris,' she said as he wound the car window down.

As the two men had shook hands, Suzette said, 'Were you coming to see me?'

'I was but I can see you're busy,' Pascal said. 'I'll leave you to enjoy your evening.' He nodded at Malik and gave Suzette a swift glance before driving away.

Dismayed, Suzette stared after him. What was that all about? Malik, still holding her hand, tugged her gently forward. She sighed. Next time she saw Pascal she would have to make a point of telling him she and Malik were old friends and nothing more. The incident made her even crosser with Malik for turning up so unexpectedly and she jerked her hand out of his.

'How long have you hired the boat for?' she asked as they approached the barge, which had passed safely through the lock and was tied up alongside.

'Depends on you,' Malik said. 'I have the possibility of extending the hire if I want to.'

Stepping on board, Suzette followed Malik along the deck to where a table and two chairs had been placed. A bottle of champagne was already nestling in an ice bucket. She looked at Malik and raised her eyebrows. 'Are we celebrating something?'

He shrugged his shoulders. 'We could be.' He poured two glasses and handed her one. '*Santé*. So tell me, has burying yourself away from everyone down here helped you to think?'

'Yes,' Suzette said. 'Most things are a lot clearer in my mind now, although I still have one major decision to make.' She watched the bubbles in her glass before raising her head and looking at Malik directly. 'Where I live when I'm no longer dancing.'

'You'll stay in Paris, surely,' Malik said. He waved his hand around at the surrounding countryside. 'I mean this is lovely for getting away from it all, but I can't see you living here. You're a Parisian through and through.'

Suzette was silent. She'd always believed that of herself too, until recently. Now she wasn't sure it was true.

'Besides,' Malik continued, 'if you like the idea I've researched for you, you'll need to be near a big city, with an airport for easy travelling. If not Paris then maybe Lille or Strasbourg. Nice could work too, but that's about it.'

'So what's your idea?'

'Photography. As in, you specialise in photos connected with the world of ballet and publish a coffee-table book of glossy photos. I've run the idea past the major theatre companies all over the country and they're willing to give you backstage permits and unlimited access to everything and everybody involved. They'd also use your work for promotion — brochures, posters, that kind of thing. Well?' Malik looked at her expectantly.

'It's a good idea,' Suzette said. 'I did think about becoming a professional photographer but hadn't considered the dance theatre aspect of things.'

'You don't sound that enthused,' Malik said. 'You would at least still be involved in the world of dance.'

Suzette nodded. 'That's the thing. I'm not sure I want to stay involved in the world of ballet when I retire. A completely different life is beginning to look more and more attractive.'

'Doing what?' Malik demanded.

'Haute couture embroidery.' *And maybe having a family if I've not left it too late* flashed into her mind.

A few seconds of silence greeted her words before Malik nodded slowly. 'That would work. You're an expert at it. But surely you'd need to be in Paris to source materials and customers?'

'I have a few customers already who I'm sure will help spread the word for me. And just because I won't be living in Paris doesn't mean I can't visit for shopping and seeing people.'

'True.' Malik picked up his knife and began to spread some pâté on a crispbread one of the boat crew had placed on the table. 'So, when are you planning to return to Paris and prepare for the final show? Sometime in the next couple of weeks I hope.'

When Suzette didn't answer immediately, he sighed. 'There's something else you've not yet told me.'

'I'm . . . I'm not sure I want to dance *Swan Lake* again,' Suzette said. 'I'm frightened. What if it goes wrong and I injure myself again? Last year's performance was an acclaimed triumph, as you know. Perhaps it would be better to leave the public with that memory.'

Malik's eyes narrowed. 'Your ankle is completely fit again, yes? And we're talking here about a role you've made your own down the years, but now you're afraid to dance it?'

Suzette nodded.

'You're also willing to forgo that last round of applause, the last of the bouquets, the last standing ovation for your performance? You want to let me down? Have me offer the role to Donna?'

'I don't want to let you down, Malik, but — '

'Then don't. I'll give you another week to decide whether you want a proper finale to your dancing career or not. Your choice.'

Suzette bit her lip. She knew she was taking the coward's way out by not taking a decision right now and telling Malik, but there was still that little knot of uncertainty in her stomach.

*   *   *

Evie pushed hanger after hanger aside on the wardrobe rail, unable to decide which outfit would be suitable for Madame de Guesclin's dinner party. The few outfits she'd brought back with her to Brittany hadn't been selected to impress with their designer labels, so of course the one dress ideally suited to tonight's dinner was still hanging in her apartment in Paris. In truth, she hadn't expected to be doing any socialising on the kind of grand scale she suspected this evening would be.

If only she'd thought about it earlier, she could have gone to the nearest town and bought something new instead of spending the last two days with Malik mooching around. But then he would have been even more grumpy than he currently was over the fact she wasn't spending this evening with him.

'Can't you cancel it? Go another evening? I'm sure Madame whatever-her-name-is would understand the unexpected appearance of an old friend?'

Evie had shaken her head. Madame de Guesclin was far more likely to regard it as being terribly bad-mannered to do such a thing unless it was an emergency. Besides, she was looking forward to seeing Pascal again.

'You could always ask if you could bring a friend,' Malik suggested hopefully. 'I quite fancy an evening socialising with the locals.'

Evie had shaken her head again. 'No, Malik. Apart from anything else I couldn't trust you not to let slip to them who I really am.'

Malik held his hands up in protest. 'I promise to keep your secret.'

'I'll book you in at the auberge for dinner. You can socialise with Libby,' Evie said.

'Not afraid I'll tell her your secret then?'

Evie glared at him. 'Don't even think about it.' No point in telling him Libby already knew. Best to let Malik think nobody but he knew who she was.

When he finally admitted defeat and left her to get ready, Evie had heaved a sigh of relief. Now, with just half an hour left before Pascal arrived to collect her, she desperately needed to find something to wear.

In the end she settled for her long

scarlet boho skirt with its asymmetric hemline teamed with her favourite pale pink silk shirt and her strappy sandals. Not her normal going-out-to-dinner wear, but her embroidered bolero simply thrown over her shoulders should add a degree of glamour. Unconventional for a posh dinner, but it was the best she could do.

Thankfully the village shop had a section devoted to handmade chocolates and Evie had managed to find a box, now wrapped in gold paper and tied with a bow that would, she hoped, make an adequate hostess present.

Pascal when he arrived kissed her on both cheeks before saying, 'You look lovely.'

Blushing, Evie said, 'Thank you. I'm not sure what your mother and her friends will make of this outfit, but I haven't brought anything that counts as dressy with me.'

Driving along the canal path, Pascal glanced at the barge. 'How is your friend?'

'Enjoying his holiday I think,' Evie

replied. 'I've shown him a few of the local sights. Tomorrow I think he goes to Vannes to meet with another friend.'

'You are going too?'

Evie shook her head. '*Non*. I have other things I need to do.'

'He leaves soon?'

Evie shrugged. 'I do not know his plans but I suspect he will have to return to Paris soon.' She turned to look out of the car window. 'It's so beautiful here. And unbelievably peaceful.'

Hydrangeas in full flower were visible everywhere as Pascal turned into the house drive and parked alongside a highly polished Mercedes sports car and an ordinary-looking saloon.

'Ah, everybody is here,' Pascal said, taking her by the hand. 'Evie, I very much hope you will enjoy this evening,' he said, a serious note in his voice. 'My mother can be, let's say intimidating, but it's important to me the two of you get on.'

Before Evie could ask why, the door opened and Madame de Guesclin was welcoming them, and ushering them into a large drawing room. 'A champagne aperitif while we get to know each other,' she said. 'And then Marie will serve dinner.'

Two women and three men were introduced to Evie in rapid succession and she was instructed to call Madame de Guesclin by her Christian name, a regal-sounding Marquisa which actually suited her. Evie smiled at everyone, handed over the chocolates and took a large gulp of her champagne cocktail. She needed some Dutch courage for what she was sure was going to turn into a long evening.

Dinner was served in a room overlooking the mature gardens. In deference to the warm summer evening, the two pairs of French doors were wide open, their delicate muslin curtains fluttering in the breeze as the perfume of the jasmine covering the loggia wafted in. Evie would have loved to have been dining out on the terrace itself, but clearly Marquisa wasn't an al fresco dining type of woman.

Thankfully she was seated with Pascal on her right and a woman on her left called Jeanette Doaré. Jeanette turned out to be the newly elected mayor of the local village and a lover of live theatre, particularly Parisian live theatre.

'Sadly these days it is not possible for Marquisa and I to go more than twice a year. We go again this September. Already we argue over which show we shall visit. *Peut-être* you will recommend one?'

Evie tensed as in the silence that followed Jeanette's question, everybody looked at her expectedly. 'I'm afraid I'm not sure which plays will still be running later in the year,' she said. 'But I'm sure you'll be spoilt for choice.'

Marie appeared at that moment with the fish course and the theatre conversation petered out, much to Evie's relief. 'I think you are very brave going into politics,' she said to Jeanette. 'How do you cope with all the criticism people throw at you when they don't like what you do?'

'People are entitled to their own opinions. They can always join the council too and try to change things.' She took a drink of the wine that Pascal was pouring for everyone before continuing. 'I have to admit I have a very thick skin these days. Disagreement with policies is one thing. It's when it gets personal that it begins to hurt.'

An animated discussion followed, led by Leon, Jeanette's husband, who clearly disliked his wife's job. Evie, pleased the conversation had moved away from Paris-related things, relaxed as she listened to the to-ing and fro-ing between the friends.

Marquisa stood up. 'Liqueurs and coffee on the terrace I think.'

'*Ca va?*' Pascal whispered in Evie's ear as she slipped her arms into her bolero jacket before dutifully following Marquisa. 'Tonight is OK for you?'

She smiled at him and nodded. 'The food is delicious. Make sure you tell Marie how much I enjoyed it all.'

Refusing a liqueur, she accepted a demitasse of coffee from Marquisa who handing it to her said, 'Pascal tells me an old friend of yours has turned up? In a barge.'

Evie nodded. 'Just for a few days.' Pascal had been talking to his mother about her? Not for the first time that evening, Evie felt uncomfortable. There was a certain undercurrent here, as if everybody apart from her was in on some gigantic secret.

'He is a close friend?' Marquisa asked.

'Yes, I have known him a long time,' Evie said, waiting for the next inevitable question, but Pascal rescued her from his mother's interrogation as he drew attention to her bolero.

'Mama, have you seen the exquisite embroidery on Evie's jacket? Isn't she clever?'

Marquisa nodded. 'She's very talented,' she added slowly.

Evie shot an unhappy glance at Pascal, willing him to pick up on it. She could have kissed him when he did.

'Mama, I've forgotten to collect some papers from the garden centre which I need to check before seeing the accountant tomorrow, so if you'll excuse us, I'll take Evie home at the same time.'

'Surely Evie can wait here while you run down to the centre,' Marquisa protested.

'I don't want to put Pascal to the trouble of making two journeys,' Evie said quickly. 'Thank you so much for this evening. And do thank Marie for the delicious food.'

'I hope to see you again before you return to Paris,' Marquisa said. 'Do feel free to call in any time.'

'Thank you,' Evie said. Calling in on Marquisa unexpectedly without a formal invitation being issued was as likely to happen as her being offered a new contract as principal dancer at the Paris Opera. It wasn't that Marquisa had been unfriendly — she had been a gracious hostess in the main — but once or twice there had been an undercurrent of something unspoken in the glances exchanged between Marquisa and Jeanette.

'I did warn you my mother can be intimidating,' Pascal said as they drove towards the auberge. 'And tonight she was on top form. My father was always trying to get her to stop being so forceful. He was always telling her, 'Let people see the gentler, kinder side of you.' I hope this evening wasn't too difficult for you.'

Evie was silent, not knowing how to answer him truthfully. Had he noticed the way innocent sentences had left unanswered questions in the air? Had he been aware of an interrogation atmosphere around the table at certain moments?

'She must be lonely now your father has died,' she said finally.

Pascal smiled ruefully. 'She is. But determined to carry on as if nothing has changed. When you get to know her better, I'm sure you'll find her to be one of the kindest people you've ever met.'

24

Libby

Two days later, the barge was still moored up near the auberge when Lucas arrived to see Libby. Since she'd had lunch with him and Veronique, Lucas had started to call in to see her most evenings after the surgery had closed. The nights he didn't arrive there was always a phone call saying he'd been called out or surgery had overrun, and a sense of disappointment running through Libby.

Lucas glanced across at the barge. 'He's still here then? Any idea who he is?'

Libby nodded and opened her mouth to say, 'It's her ex-dancing partner applying pressure for Evie to return to Paris to prepare for her last ballet before she retires.' She closed her mouth again quickly. She couldn't say

292

that because Lucas didn't know Evie's secret. And she'd promised not to tell anyone. 'Just a friend. I think he's leaving tomorrow,' she said instead.

'Pascal will be pleased,' Lucas said. 'I saw him today and he asked if I knew what was going on. It's not like him to want gossip about anyone. I think he likes Evie.'

'Come on, let's take supper and sit under the pergola,' Libby said, deciding a change of conversation was needed. She felt uncomfortable not being able to talk truthfully to Lucas. 'I need to talk to you about next week.'

Despite having told Helen she didn't need to make a list of guests for her party, Libby knew she had to start organising things. A to-do list would have to be written soon. 'I really don't want a fuss made,' she said now to Lucas.

'It's your birthday so do what you want,' Lucas said. 'Though personally I'm looking forward to making a fuss of you. It is a milestone birthday after all.'

'You'll be trotting out that old cliché

next, that life begins at forty,' Libby said, laughing.

'You're at the beginning of a new life over here so maybe there is some truth in that saying,' Lucas said, a serious note in his voice. Catching a hold of her hand he squeezed it, looking at her intently. 'You've already started to change your life and it will continue to change — with me in it more and more I hope.'

Libby's laughter faded away as she realised the implication behind Lucas's words. 'Oh Lucas,' she said. 'I'm not sure I'm ready.'

'You will be,' Lucas said confidently. 'First I become your best friend, and then . . . and then *voilà*, you find you can't live without me!'

The way he said *voilà* and waved his hand in the air with delight made Libby laugh again, and this time Lucas joined in before saying seriously, 'I mean it, Libby. Soon friendship alone won't be enough for me. I want to look after you. To love you.'

'Lucas, I don't know what to say,' Libby said softly.

'Say nothing. Just think about it. Now I must go.' With a fleeting kiss, he left.

Later as she prepared for bed, Libby thought about his words, and then about her life with Dan before she came to France. When Dan died she'd believed her life was over and she'd never find love again, but here was Lucas professing love and wanting her to be in his life. Admittedly the thought of being part of a couple again, especially with Lucas, was exciting. The days she didn't see him always seemed so empty, as if there was something missing. Something — or somebody.

Was it too soon, though? She'd barely spent a summer in France and had known Lucas for only a few short months. Was it long enough to acknowledge that yes, she would like to think of a future with him? And Chloe — how would she react?

The next morning as Libby cleared the kitchen after serving breakfast to the guests, she glimpsed Evie standing by the canal path waving goodbye as Malik's barge started to make its way back upstream. Guessing that Evie would walk up to the auberge afterwards, Libby turned to put the coffee on just as the phone rang.

'Odette. How's the holiday? And the packing?'

'The holiday was wonderful,' Odette said. 'We should finish the packing soon. Then we come home in time for your party.'

'Good. I've missed having you here,' Libby said.

'Is Evie still with you?' Odette asked.

'Yes. She seems happy living in the gîte, although . . . ' Libby hesitated before adding, ' . . . she's had a friend turn up unexpectedly, which has made her tense. Why d'you ask?'

'I discovered something recently. I'll

tell you when I get back,' Odette said. 'See you soon.'

Briefly Libby wondered if it were possible Odette had stumbled across Evie's real identity. If she had, and intended to challenge Evie, Libby prayed Evie wouldn't assume she'd broken her promise and given the secret away.

A knock on the kitchen door and Evie appeared. 'You look a bit frazzled,' Libby said. 'Coffee?' Without waiting for an answer she poured one and handed it to Evie.

'Thanks. Malik has reiterated his ultimatum: Decide whether or not I return to dance *Swan Lake* one last time,' she said, looking at Libby. 'You'd think it would be an easy decision.' She shook her head. 'Part of me says dance. Another part says retire gracefully and start my new life. I have to ring him by the end of the week.'

'Only you can decide,' Libby said.

Evie nodded. 'I know. Have you seen anything of Pascal? I haven't heard from him since the evening I had dinner with him and his mother.'

Libby shook her head. 'No. He was asking Lucas about Malik though. Wondering if he knew what was going on. How was the dinner, by the way?'

'Dinner was . . . dinner was tricky for some reason. I must ring Pascal and arrange to meet up. But first I have to decide what I'm going to do.'

'Evie . . . ' Libby hesitated. 'You know I promised to keep your secret? I promise you I have, but Odette is due home soon and from the conversation I've just had with her, I've a funny feeling she knows you're not who you say you are. So it's make up your mind time on all fronts.'

25

Evie

Evie paid the taxi driver and stepped out onto the car park above the pépinère and slowly began to make her way towards the entrance. Intent on buying a plant for Libby's birthday, she hoped Pascal would be at work and he'd be able to advise her on which kind of plant would thrive in Libby's garden.

She wanted to talk to him too. Tell him she was no longer at a crossroads in her life. To see his reaction when she told him the road she would take in the future had been decided.

The pépinère was far bigger than Evie expected and busy with people wandering around under the huge glass roof that covered a vast area with hundreds of different plants under its protective covering. Seven huge poly-tunnels were placed around the land with gardeners tending plants and advising people on their choices. Where to start looking?

Lola raced towards her and she bent down to stroke the dog. 'Do you greet everyone like this, Lola? Or do you remember me?'

'Evie?'

She straightened up and smiled at Pascal, who was regarding her quizzically.

'Have you come to see me?'

'Yes, and I also need help in choosing something for Libby's birthday,' Evie said.

'We'll do that first then. Tree? Shrub? Smaller plants?'

'I've always adored magnolia trees,' Evie said. 'I think one in the auberge garden would look beautiful.'

'*Bon*. Magnolias are down the far end,' Pascal said. 'Follow me.'

It took some time to reach the tree and shrub section of the pépinère as several customers stopped Pascal to ask his advice, which he gave with his usual calm and courteous manner. Evie watched while he was talking and realised how completely at home he was here, his shyness forgotten as he explained how different plants needed certain things from the soil. How and when to prune an orchard was another question he answered expertly before they reached the tree section.

'You love your work, don't you?' she said as another happy customer wandered away.

Pascal nodded. 'Up until now it's been my life. Right, here are the magnolias.' He stood and carefully looked at the trees in their pots. 'You don't want one that's too small or too big. Ah, this one is perfect.' He pulled one forward. 'Big enough to flower next year and small enough to have some growing to do before pruning.'

'Can you deliver it for me?' Evie asked.

'Of course. Right, that's Libby's present taken care of. Now we talk,'

Pascal said. 'We'll go to my cabin. We won't be disturbed there.'

The cabin, hidden away behind the main office, had a desk with paperwork piled high over it and a tray of seedlings perched on top. Lola made for her basket under the desk and Pascal closed the door behind them.

'Has Malik gone back to Paris?' he asked.

'A couple of days ago,' Evie said. She looked at Pascal. 'He's a good friend. We go back a long way.' She fiddled with the strap of her watch before saying, 'You know I was at a crossroads in my life? Well, he was a part of it.'

'Are you and he more than friends?' Pascal said.

Evie shook her head. 'No. We're close friends but never anything more.'

'You were holding hands.'

'As friends.' Evie took a deep breath. Time to tell Pascal the truth. 'Pascal, I'm not really Evie Patem. Well I am, sort of, but my real name is — '

'Suzette Shelby, and you're an

internationally famous ballet dancer,' Pascal finished for her. 'And Malik was your dance partner before he became a choreographer.'

Evie's mouth opened in surprise as she stared at him. 'How did you know? Libby? She promised not to tell anyone.'

Pascal shook his head. 'My mother. I had my suspicions from the first time I met you that you weren't who you said you were. Mother confirmed it when she met you, and Malik turning up was another big clue. An unusual name and one my mother knew.'

Evie could only stare at him, speechless. Now she knew the reason behind those awkward silences at dinner. Marquisa de Guesclin and her friends had known who she was all the time.

'My mother has always adored the ballet and frequently goes to Paris. She says you dance exquisitely. She likens you to Violette Verdy at her best.'

Evie smiled. 'My mother would have adored hearing that. It was always her ambition for me to be up with the best French dancers. Verdy, Sylvie Guillem. . . Personally I always wanted to be Lesley Caron.'

'So has being Evie Patem and staying in Brittany helped you make a plan for the future?' Pascal asked quietly.

'Yes. Now my dancing days are coming to an end I intend to make a new career for myself with embroidery and haute couture.' She paused. 'I'm also going to leave Paris and move to Brittany.'

Pascal gave her a broad smile. 'Truly?'

Evie nodded. 'Of course I have to find somewhere permanent to live and . . . ' She hesitated. 'I'd really like to stay as Evie, but Libby has already pointed out the difficulties with doing that. So at some point I have to let it be known I am Suzette Shelby.' She sighed. 'Then the media circus will hit town I expect.'

Pascal dismissed that with a wave of his hand. 'Pff. A week or two and then somebody else will be in the news.'

'I hope you're right,' Evie said. 'I've loved being Evie. I wish I could stay with her really.'

'You'll always be Evie to me,' Pascal said. 'Although my mother will probably insist on calling you Suzette. She'll be over the moon that I've fallen in love with someone famous.'

'Fallen in love with?' Evie whispered as Pascal took her gently in his arms and kissed her.

It was minutes later when Evie stood back and looked at Pascal. 'I've still got to phone Malik tonight and tell him that I'm not dancing *Swan Lake* this autumn. I think he's expecting the news but I know he'll be cross and disappointed.'

Pascal took hold of her hands. 'Would you dance it this last time for me? I'd love to see you dance.'

'You would? But what if I have another injury? I know it's only a week of performances. But what if — '

Pascal silenced her with his finger

across her lips. 'Shh. Life is full of what-ifs. I just think you need to bring the curtain down on your dancing career properly, not just fade away.'

Evie looked at him silently as Pascal took his phone out of his pocket and handed it to her. 'Phone Malik and tell him your decision. You'll dance for him one more time. Not just for him, but for me and you too.'

Evie smiled at him as she took the phone. Pascal was right: allowing the curtain to fall after a final week of dancing, and saying a proper farewell to her old life, could only be a liberating experience. One that would leave her free to pursue her new life without regrets.

26

Libby

Libby woke early the morning of her birthday and lay in bed for a few moments, planning her day. The season was almost over but there were still guests booked in, so first there would be breakfasts to organise and then other routine tasks to do before she turned her mind to tonight's party: canapés to organise, salads and side dishes to be made, champagne bottles to be placed in the fridge, meat to be marinated for the barbecue. Her hair needed washing too.

Lucas had promised to pop in sometime during the day and set up his music system ready for the party. He'd also been talking about bringing some fairy lights to thread through the trees. Libby smiled to herself as Lucas entered her thoughts. Over the summer their lives had definitely become more and more entwined, almost without her realising. It was good having a man in her life again, especially someone as special as him.

Flinging back the duvet, Libby slid out of bed. One of the things she must do this weekend was to talk to Chloe while she was here. See how she felt about Lucas, and whether it would be a problem for her if their friendship became something deeper.

Odette arrived unexpectedly mid-morning, clutching a jar of delicate rose-petal confiture and some lavender Marseille soap which she handed to Libby. 'These are just presents I thought you'd like from our holiday. They are not for your birthday,' she explained earnestly. 'We'll bring that with us this evening.'

'Thank you,' Libby said, sniffing the soap. 'This smells wonderful. You had a good time?'

Odette nodded. 'Amazing. And now

we've come back to help Isabelle get her new home ready. The notaire, he say another fortnight and it will be hers.'

'Brilliant,' Libby said. 'So pleased things are working out well for her.'

'Is Evie around?' Odette asked.

'I think she went out earlier. Did you want to see her?'

Odette shook her head. '*Non.*' She hesitated before continuing. 'Has she told you yet what she does in Paris? Only, I don't think Evie Patem is her real name. I think she's the missing ballerina Suzette Shelby.'

Libby sighed inwardly, her promise to Evie not to break her confidence foremost in her mind. 'Why d'you think that?'

'A photograph of Suzette in a newspaper saying she was still missing,' Odette said. 'I'm sure it was her. Next time I see Evie I'm going to ask her.'

'If she is Suzette Shelby, don't you think she called herself Evie for a reason — to have some privacy?' Libby said. 'She's not hurting anyone by having a pseudonym. Perhaps she'll tell us herself one day. Anyway, I like her whatever her name.'

Odette looked at her. 'You don't seem surprised. In fact, it's almost as if you knew.'

Libby bit her lip. There was no way she was going to break her promise to Evie and confirm to Odette that Evie was indeed Suzette.

Before she could answer, Helen bustled into the kitchen and Libby smothered a sigh of relief. Since she and Peter had arrived yesterday, Helen had been in major bossy mode as regards the party. Libby had been relieved to see that Peter was the most relaxed she'd seen him for years. Helen had clearly had words.

Libby smiled, grateful for the interruption. Now she wouldn't have to deny or confirm Odette's theory. She hoped and prayed Odette wouldn't choose the party this evening to challenge Evie.

'Libby, Peter wants to know if you have any outdoor fairy lights? If not you'll have to go and buy some. Oh, and charcoal for the barbecue?'

'Lucas is bringing lights over later when he drops the music system off,' Libby said. 'The barbecue charcoal is in the shed at the back.'

'Right. I hope Chloe gets here soon. I need her to do something for me.'

'Can't I help?' Libby said, but Helen had vanished as quickly as she'd appeared.

Libby glanced at her watch. Chloe had said she and her friend were catching the overnight ferry, so in theory she — they — could be here any time now.

The noise of a powerful motorbike driving into the auberge parking area caught her attention and she went to the front door. There weren't any guests booked in to arrive today and she was full anyway, so these tourists were going to be unlucky if they were looking to stay at the auberge.

'Hi, Mum. Happy birthday,' Chloe called out as she took off her helmet and shook her hair free before swinging her leg over and stepping off the bike.

Chloe had come on the back of a motorbike?

'You hate bikes,' Libby said, bemused as she watched a fair-haired man carefully balance his helmet on the wide handle bars and headlamp before leaping off the bike. Behind her Libby was conscious of Odette starting to laugh.

'You said nothing would ever get you on the back of one,' Libby said.

'*Incroyable* what love will do,' Odette whispered. 'I'll see you tonight. *À tout à l'heure.*'

'Bye,' Libby answered automatically, turning to hug Chloe.

'Hi, Chloe's Mum. I'm Alex.'

'Pleased to meet you, Alex,' Libby said, shaking his hand.

'Mum, we're starving. Can I rustle us up something to eat?'

'Help yourselves. Look out for Aunty Helen though — she has plans for you!'

Libby turned as she heard more vehicles on the canal path. She watched as Lucas drove in followed closely by Pascal in the pépinère lorry. 'We're going to run out of parking spaces at this rate,' she said as Lucas leant in to kiss her.

'Pascal, what are you doing here?'

'Delivering your birthday present from Evie and me. I'd ask you where you'd like me to plant it but will you trust me to put it in the best place?'

Libby nodded. 'You're the expert. Is it a magnolia tree? Wonderful. I've always wanted one of those.'

'I've brought the lights and the music,' Lucas said. 'I can set the music up later but right now I have to dash back to the clinic, so if Peter could do the lights?'

'I'll tell him. Maybe he can rope Alex in to help,' Libby said. 'I'm still stunned about that,' she said, shaking her head as she pointed at the red-and-cream machine.

The rest of the day was equally busy and passed in a flash for Libby. At six o'clock Helen insisted she go up to her apartment, have a long soak in the bath, and get ready for her party. 'Don't come downstairs again a minute before eight o'clock. No, actually — stay there until someone fetches you.'

'There's still a lot to do,' Libby protested.

'Nothing that we can't cope with,' Helen said. 'Go. And no peeking out of the window! Close the shutters!'

★   ★   ★

Libby did as she was told and enjoyed the rare opportunity to take a long soak in a perfumed bath before changing into her sparkly party dress and waiting to be summoned downstairs. For the last half hour there had been very little noise in the house, so she assumed party preparations were finished and everyone else was now getting ready.

Five past eight and the door opened. 'Mum, are you ready? It's time to party,' Chloe said.

'Before we go downstairs, tell me something,' Libby said. 'Are you serious about Alex?'

314

Chloe nodded. 'Yes. I know you'll love him too when you know him.' She looked at her mother. 'My turn. Are you serious about Lucas?'

Libby blushed. 'I could be, if that's all right with you.'

'Mum, it's nothing to do with me, so long as you're happy.'

Libby nodded. 'I didn't want you thinking that I was forgetting about your dad. I'll never do that. I was also afraid you might resent me meeting someone new.'

'Mum, I want you to be happy. Lucas is a lovely man, different from Dad but just as nice,' Chloe said, hugging her. 'Come on, birthday girl. Let's go down.'

With fairy lights strung through the trees, tall Chinese candles dotted around, and a Nat King Cole song floating on the air, the auberge terrace and garden had been transformed. To Libby's embarrassment, as she appeared everyone burst into song and 'Happy Birthday' temporarily drowned out Nat King Cole.

Libby smiled as Evie and Pascal

315

made their way over to her at the end of the song. 'You've taken your wig off.'

'Pascal persuaded me it was time. I'm hoping people here will still treat me like Evie though, rather than Suzette.'

'I promise I will,' Libby said.

Later, when the barbecue was dying down and the food had been eaten, Lucas appeared at her side and took her by the hand. 'My present is in your shed. Come with me to fetch it?'

Quietly pushing open the shed door, Lucas led her over to the corner where a young black-and-white dog was curled up sleeping. 'It's the little one we helped deliver,' Libby whispered as the dog opened her eyes and cautiously thumped her tail.

Lucas nodded. 'All the others have gone to be farm dogs, but this one was kept back especially for you. For us.'

Libby bent down and stroked the dog. 'She's beautiful. Does she have a name yet?'

'*Non*. As she's going to be your dog, I thought you should be the one to name her,' Lucas said quietly.

Libby was quiet for a moment, intent on stroking the dog, before looking up at Lucas and saying, 'How do you feel about calling her Hope?'

Lucas smiled as he pulled her to her feet and took her into his arms. 'Perfect. We have Hope for our future together.'

27

Odette

Settling back into a routine after their holiday in the south of France was easier than Odette expected. Having Isabelle living with them was wonderful. The old mas was finally becoming her home with the promise of happy family times to come.

Part of her routine now involved walking to the village boulangerie for croissants every morning before returning for breakfast under the loggia. It was amazing how many friends she bumped into — friends she'd seen infrequently when she'd been running the auberge. Retiring to the village had been a good idea of Bruno's after all. Life was good.

Isabelle's morning sickness was slowly disappearing and she, too, was settling happily into her new way of life. Because the house she was buying was empty and the formalities were proceeding quickly, Isabelle was able to have access and to make a start on getting things ready to move in.

Bruno set to work clearing the garden overgrowth, cutting back brambles and pruning large lilac trees and rhododendron bushes. Odette mowed the lawn and organised some pots for the patio by the kitchen door.

'You will be needing some outdoor chairs and a table,' she said.

'Amongst other things,' Isabelle replied. 'The list is getting longer by the day. There's a large *vide grenier* this Sunday in Carhaix. Shall we go and see what we can find?'

Odette nodded. 'Hopefully there will be a bargain or two there.'

Bruno declined to join them Sunday morning, which didn't surprise Odette. 'You know he's never been one for this sort of thing,' she said to Isabelle as she slipped into the driving seat of their car.

'Remember how he'd do anything to avoid the *vide greniers* your school held to raise funds?'

Isabelle laughed. 'He was ace at making those wooden reindeers out of logs for sale at the Christmas bazaars though. Everyone wanted one.'

The streets where the *vide grenier* was being held were buzzing with busy stalls and people wandering around clutching recently acquired treasures. Isabelle soon spotted a stand selling new and almost-new baby equipment and the two of them spent an enjoyable half hour selecting things. Walking back to put their purchases in the car, Isabelle's mobile rang at the same moment Odette saw Lucas striding towards them.

'Thank goodness I've found you,' Lucas said. 'Odette, I'm sorry but Bruno has been taken ill.' He glanced at Isabelle, listening intently to a message on her phone. 'That will be Libby.'

'What's happened?' Odette asked, trying to stop her voice trembling.

'Bruno had a suspected heart attack about half an hour ago.' Lucas put an arm around Odette's shoulders. 'I'd rung him to talk about the motorcycle club meeting next week when I heard him collapse. Luckily I managed to alert the pompiers and they were there in minutes. He's in hospital now.'

'I must go to him,' Odette said. 'Which hospital?'

'For the moment the one here in town, as it was the nearest. I'll drive you,' Lucas said. He glanced across at Isabelle. 'You OK?' Isabelle nodded. 'Libby said she'd wait at the hospital until we get there.'

Libby was waiting outside the main hospital entrance when Lucas drove up and hurried over to them. 'Not being a relative, I haven't been allowed in to see him, but they've said he's stable,' she told Odette and Isabelle. 'You can go straight up.'

Libby watched the two of them disappear into the hospital before turning to Lucas. 'If you hadn't phoned

Bruno when you did . . . ' She shook her head. 'It doesn't bear thinking about.'

'Then don't,' Lucas said. 'Just pray that we got him here in time.'

28

Evie

Since telling Malik she'd dance *Swan Lake*, and swearing him to secrecy over the fact it would be the last time ever, Evie knew she had to begin her serious exercise routine again. She'd neglected it over the summer, doing only the minimum to keep herself flexible, but now she had to ease herself back into the demanding routine that had been a part of her life for so many years.

The main problem, though, was finding a space to actually dance in. The gîte chairs with a pole secured between them were adequate for exercising, although a large mirror so she could check her positions were correct would have been nice.

Malik phoned every day. His constant refrain was, 'Please return to

Paris. Everything is here for you.'

'I'll be back for the start of the official rehearsals,' Evie said. 'But I really want to stay here for as long as I can. There are a few things to sort out for when I return. Finding somewhere permanent to live, for a start.'

Libby had said she was welcome to rent the gîte for as long as she liked; but while it was big enough to live in, running a haute couture business from there was not possible.

'The thing is,' she said to Pascal one evening as they sat outside the gîte enjoying a salad supper Evie had prepared, 'I'm afraid Malik's right. I desperately need space to dance in.' She sighed. 'I think I have to go back to Paris soon. I'm beginning to wish I hadn't agreed to dance again. That I could simply stay here and get on with my new life.'

Pascal took hold of her hand. 'But then I wouldn't have the pleasure of seeing you perform, which I am very much looking forward to. Afterwards, I promise you'll feel free . . . free as a papillon to fly back to me.' He bent down to give Lola, curled up at his feet, a stroke before asking, 'If you had somewhere to dance, you stay for how long?'

'Two, maybe three more weeks. Then I'd have ten days with the company up in Paris before opening night.'

Pascal nodded thoughtfully. '*D'accord.* Tomorrow evening I take you to look at a place.'

Evie looked at him hopefully. 'You know somewhere? Only the floor will have to be good, like a stage floor.'

'That is why I need to look before taking you to see.'

Evie smiled at him before gently leaning in and kissing his cheek. '*Merci.*'

An hour later as she waved Pascal goodbye, she found herself praying that wherever Pascal had in mind would be possible. The thought of having to drag herself back to Paris early, not seeing Pascal for weeks and leaving the beginnings of her new life here, wasn't something she even wanted to think about.

'I do so hope I can use this room

Pascal thinks will be suitable,' she said to Libby the next morning. 'I feel so comfortable here. Paris . . . ' She shrugged. 'It no longer feels like my home. I know going back will only be temporary, but I wish it wasn't necessary.'

Libby smiled sympathetically. 'I understand. When I'd made the decision to buy the auberge, I just wanted it to happen instantly.'

'Have you heard how Bruno is?' Evie asked.

'Odette says he should be home next week, with a diet sheet and instructions to take it easy.'

Evie's mobile on the table between them beeped. 'Excuse me for a moment; it's Pascal.'

'This evening I collect you at seven o'clock and show you the floor I promised you. I think it is good. Then we walk Lola.' He hesitated before adding, 'And then my mother has asked us to have supper with her.'

'Just us? Not any of her friends this time? OK. See you later,' Evie said, pulling a face at Libby as she pressed the off switch.

'Problem?' Libby asked.

'Marquisa has issued a supper invitation for this evening.' She sighed. 'I hope it's nothing like her dinner party.'

* * *

Evie climbed into Pascal's Land Rover that evening to be greeted affectionately by both Pascal and Lola. Pascal, she was relieved to see, was casually dressed in jeans and a pale blue linen shirt. Hopefully this meant her own casual outfit of white cropped trousers and a Breton sweatshirt would pass tonight's supper dress code.

Pascal surprised her by driving straight to his home, but instead of parking he drove on round to the back of the house and followed another track for a short distance before stopping in front of a stone barn out of sight of the main house.

'My father used this as his studio and

as the estate office. Me, I do not need a studio and I prefer my office in the pépinière.' Turning a key in the large wooden door, he pushed it open and Evie stepped inside.

The empty interior stretched away from her for 40 feet with a high, black-beamed open ceiling, but it was the wooden floor that made her gasp with delight.

'This is perfect,' she said, smiling at Pascal. 'If I can rig up a barre as well, I can practise everything I need to in here. My pointe work, bourrée and all les fouetté I'll need for *Swan Lake*.' She did an experimental twirl into the middle of the barn. 'The space is wonderful.'

'And afterwards you use it for your business, yes? We can fit it out with shelves and tables — even a small boutique at one end.'

'Really? Marquisa would let me?'

'Of course. She suggested it.' Pascal looked at his watch. 'Time to walk Lola before supper.' Locking the barn behind them, Evie followed Pascal down the path towards a small wood before a stretch of open countryside.

'This is your land?' she asked, as Pascal threw a ball for Lola to chase and fetch.

Pascal nodded. 'I rent it out to a local farmer these days.'

'How much land do you actually have?' Evie suspected Pascal and his mother were wealthier than she'd thought.

'Now, about 3000 hectares. We sold some off when my father died to pay tax and things. Ideally I'd like to sell about half of what's left; the pépinère is enough for me but Mother won't hear of it.'

Marquisa was waiting for them when they returned to the house. 'Suzette, welcome,' she said, kissing Evie on both cheeks. 'I was hoping you'd call in and see me after the dinner party, but Pascal he tells me you have been busy.'

'There is a lot to sort before I return to Paris,' Evie said, resisting the urge to tell Marquisa to please call her Evie. She'd only ignore the instruction anyway if what Pascal had said was correct.

'You like the barn? It is suitable for you to practise dancing in?'

'Thank you. It's perfect.'

'I am so thrilled you are going to be part of our family,' Marquisa said. 'But Pascal tells me I'm not allowed to tell my friends yet. He says I have to wait until after you dance.' She raised an eyebrow quizzically. '*Peut-être* you give me permission?'

Evie shook her head. She and Pascal had decided together to try and keep their relationship secret and out of the media until after *Swan Lake*. 'Please keep the secret for a little longer, until after *Swan Lake*.'

'Pascal has organised tickets for the last night,' Marquisa said. 'It's going to be wonderful watching my future daughter-in-law dance.'

29

Libby

Libby walked down through the village towards Odette and Bruno's, struggling to make Hope behave on the end of the lead and to stop pulling. Lucas had given her a couple of lessons and already the puppy was responding, especially when Lucas was holding the lead.

'Hope, heel,' she said sternly. Maybe it had been a mistake to bring the boisterous puppy when Bruno was only recently home. Still, it would be a quick visit; she didn't want to tire Bruno out and she also needed to get home to prepare supper. None of the auberge guests wanted dinner this evening, so she'd invited Evie and Pascal to join her and Lucas for supper.

As she struggled to open the mas

gate, holding her shopping bag containing a book and some magazines for Bruno, and Hope's lead in the same hand, Odette appeared to help.

'Bruno is in the garden,' she said.

'Not working, I hope?' Libby asked. 'How is he?'

Odette laughed. 'No, he is not working. I have him tied to a chair under the pergola! As for how he is, he does not make a good patient. But the doctors say he must take it easy for some weeks. Otherwise . . . ' She shrugged. 'I don't want another scare, so I make him behave.'

Bruno was pleased to see her and made a fuss of Hope before telling Libby to let her off the lead. 'Can't come to any harm here.'

'You're looking better,' Libby said, handing him the books and magazines. 'Sorry, I was warned chocolates weren't allowed.'

'Shame,' Bruno said. 'You could always sneak me a box later! But these look interesting. Thank you.'

'Isabelle not around today?' Libby asked.

Odette shook her head. 'She's gone to meet Laurent from Brest airport. Tomorrow they go to the notaire to finalise the house.'

'Chloe phoned last night. Her internship has finished so she'll be coming down to stay until college starts,' Libby said. 'I know she's looking forward to seeing Isabelle again.'

'You will enjoy having her here,' Odette said. 'Now the summer is finishing, you have the time to enjoy her company. Tell me Libby, the summer — how has it been for you? You like living in France? Enjoy running the auberge?'

'It's been brilliant. I'm so glad I came,' Libby said. 'I'm a bit worried about how quiet life is going to be in winter but I'm sure I'll find plenty of things to do.'

'Lucas, he will keep you from being bored,' Odette said, laughing at the look on Libby's face. 'And Evie too. How is she? Has Marquisa frightened her off Pascal?'

Libby shook her head. 'No. Marquisa

thoroughly approves of their relationship. I think she's basking in the reflected glory of having someone famous in the family.'

Bruno nodded. 'Pascal was here earlier. I've never seen him so happy.'

Later, walking home along the canal path, Libby remembered her 'it's been brilliant' response to Odette's question about enjoying life in France and the auberge. To think less than a year ago she was filled with trepidation about moving to a foreign country to start a new life on her own, wondering whether it would turn out to be a mistake and she'd end up returning a sadder and wiser woman.

Well, it hadn't been a mistake. She was definitely wiser, but sadder didn't enter into the equation. She was totally happy with the way her French life was turning out. Her French had improved no end, too, thanks to using it every day.

Lucas rang to warn her he would be late as evening surgery was busy, so as the sun set and the air turned chilly, Libby set the kitchen table for supper and placed some candles in the centre. Homemade tapina on savoury biscuits and a basket of garlic bread would keep everyone's hunger pangs at bay until Lucas arrived.

Evie was full of plans for her return to Brittany when she and Pascal walked over from the gîte.

'While I'm in Paris, Pascal is going to arrange for the conversion of the barn and I'm going to fit in as much material-buying as I can. I expect I'll have to flit back and forth for a few weeks but I can't wait to start organising things here. I'll have to sell the Paris apartment too.' Evie sighed. 'It's going to be months before everything is sorted.'

'You'll be so busy time will fly,' Libby assured her, remembering how quickly the days and weeks had gone before her own move. 'Just concentrate on one thing at a time. Dancing first, then afterwards everything else will fall into place.'

'I know you are right,' Evie said. 'I return to Paris next week to start rehearsals.'

Lucas arrived then and Libby took the large lasagne she'd made earlier out of the oven, urging everyone to help themselves.

Pascal glanced across at Libby and Lucas before saying, 'You two are coming up for the last night, aren't you? I've booked a box and arranged the tickets. I was hoping Odette would come, but she says she can't leave Bruno overnight.'

'Oh Pascal, thank you. It's a lovely idea, but — ' Libby said.

Lucas interrupted her protests. 'Definitely. Wouldn't miss it for the world.' He turned to Libby. 'Chloe will be here to take care of Hope and any late guests. Time in Paris would be perfect for our first weekend away together.'

'Please come, Libby,' Evie said quietly. 'It would be wonderful knowing my new best friend was in the audience.'

'And I long to show you the Paris I know,' Lucas said.

Libby smiled. 'How can I say no? Thank you, Pascal. We'll be there.'

30

Evie / Suzette

Evie stood on the small balcony outside her apartment, listening to the noise of the early-morning rush-hour traffic as she looked at and gently fingered the ring on the fourth finger of her left hand.

Her engagement ring from Pascal. He'd stunned her by producing it two evenings ago as they'd arrived back at the gîte after spending the evening together dining at her favourite restaurant on the lake at Huelgoat. Three large diamonds in an antique setting, it had fitted perfectly.

'It was my grandmother's. If you don't like it we can choose another one together, but I know she'd adore the thought of my wife wearing it.'

'It's beautiful,' Evie said, admiring

the way it sparkled on her finger. 'I love the fact that it's a family heirloom.'

'I know we agreed to keep things quiet until after *Swan Lake*, but I wanted to make things official between us before you disappeared back to Paris,' Pascal said quietly. 'So I bought you this as well.' He handed her a gold chain. 'If you want to keep our secret for a little longer, you can slip it on this and wear it round your neck out of sight, when you're in Paris.'

Taking the chain Evie said, 'I promise you I'll be telling everyone how lucky I am once the ballet is over, but until then, the chain is a brilliant idea. Thank you.'

The ring had stayed on her finger until she'd left Brittany yesterday, when she'd carefully placed it on the chain around her neck and hidden it under her shirt. But last night she'd taken it off the chain and replaced it on her finger. There was nobody in the apartment to see it and she loved having it on her finger. Now, though, it was time to slip it on the chain and hide it. Thankfully there were only two more weeks before she could tell the world about Pascal and place it back on her finger. Forever.

Closing the balcony doors, Evie went into her tiny kitchen to make a cup of coffee, mentally beginning to plan her day and start a to-do list. Rehearsals began tomorrow so she needed to make the most of a completely free day. Once the ballet opened there would be few hours during the day to spare, except for the two matinee days when she'd be at the theatre from midday until late evening.

One of the first things she must do was to ring Malik and tell him she was back in town, as well as make sure he remembered his promise not to tell anyone — *anyone* — that next week Suzette Shelby would be performing in her last ballet. That *Swan Lake* was to literally be her swan dance. Of course there would have to be an official announcement, but she'd make it in her own time and in her own way. No way did she want the added pressure of an announcement in the press before opening night.

An hour later with a long to-do list in front of her, Evie pressed Malik's number on her phone. It went straight to voicemail.

'Malik, I'm back in the Paris apartment. Ring me.' She pressed the end call button. Damn, she needed to know times for tomorrow so she could plan some appointments she needed to make. There was a lot to fit in this week. Thirty seconds later her phone rang.

'Welcome back to civilisation. You've been missed,' Malik said.

'Only by you I'd guess,' she said. 'Update me with what's going on, especially who's in the company for this ballet.'

Malik reeled off a couple of well-known names before saying, 'Everyone is looking forward to seeing you again. People have been wondering where you were all summer. Some thought you'd already retired.'

'I hope you disillusioned them. Malik, please tell me you haven't told anyone, particularly the press, that this ballet is to be my last public performance.'

'If people know it's their last opportunity to see Suzette Shelby dance, they'll storm the box office for tickets,' Malik protested.

'Promise me you haven't?'

Malik laughed. 'OK. I promise. There isn't a single ticket left to sell anyway. But you can't just drift away to Brittany or wherever without telling your fans.'

'I know. I'm planning to do it in my own time and in my own way,' Evie said. 'And it's definitely Brittany where I'm going, nowhere else.'

Part of her wanted to tell Malik about Pascal and her engagement, but she couldn't be sure he'd keep a second secret. Switching off her phone and moving across to the small table where she kept a few framed photographs, she picked up one of her mother. Lovingly she traced her finger over the face staring back up at her.

'If only I could tell you,' she said. 'I know you'd adore Pascal as much as I do. I so wish he could have known you too.'

She placed the photo back on the table and turned to pick up her to-do list. Phone the immobiliers to put the apartment on the market. Get to the Marché Saint-Pierre one day to stock up on some materials. Buy some jeans and a pair of sturdy shoes; she'd already ruined a favourite pair of flatties walking Lola with Pascal. So much to do.

With rehearsals every day and fitting the various appointments and shopping in, the week before opening night flew by. Thoughts of returning to Pascal and Brittany got pushed further and further away for hours on end during the day as life became more and more frantic. Thankfully apart from the occasional shooting pain, her ankle was holding up well and Evie was once again enjoying dancing.

Pascal rang every evening, keeping her up to date with his news and the progress on the barn. She didn't mention the twinges in her ankle when he asked how things were going. No way was she giving in to injury this week. However painful it became, she was determined to dance through it.

Suzette Shelby was back in town for her final curtain call. And nothing, but nothing, was going to stop her giving it her all.

31

Suzette / Evie

After a week of performances, rapturous applause and so many curtain calls she'd lost count, Suzette was on a high. As the heavy curtains swished to the floor after the final matinee performance and the applause died away, she began making her way back to the dressing room. As always, the adrenalin rush from dancing left her on a high.

Tiring as it was to give two performances a day, she'd always liked the afternoon houses. Today was no exception: an audience full of ballet-crazy girls, their exhilaration as they'd watched spellbound was palpable and had reached her across the footlights.

Malik was waiting for her in the dressing room. 'Great performance, Suzette. One of your best ever. Magical.'

Suzette smiled. 'I hope the magic stays for this evening,' she said quietly.

'You sure you want it to end this evening?' Malik said. 'I've a short season of modern ballet booked down in Nice for Christmas week.' He looked at her hopefully. 'You are so fit now, you could easily do it.'

Suzette shook her head. 'Thanks but no thanks.' She picked up the chain with her engagement ring from the drawer she'd hidden it in. Impossible to wear around her neck while performing, she'd wanted it close. She hadn't told Malik yet about her engagement.

'I'm looking forward to the next stage of my life. Tonight this goes back on my finger and is never coming off,' she said, showing Malik the ring.

'Pascal? He's a lucky man. I wish you every happiness.'

Hearing a quiet knock and the dressing-room door opening, Suzette turned. 'Libby and Lucas. How lovely. I wasn't expecting to see you until the after-show party.'

'We're not stopping,' Libby said as

they kissed cheeks. 'We don't want to disrupt your pre-show routine, but wanted you to know we've all arrived and to wish you luck.'

'Thank you. Pascal and Marquisa, where are they?'

'Gone straight to their hotel,' Lucas said. 'Pascal sends his love and he'll see you later. And so will we.' A minute later Libby and Lucas were gone, closely followed by Malik.

'Suzette, I have things to do. I'll be back in an hour.' And Malik was gone too.

Left on her own, Suzette settled down into her familiar pre-performance routine. As she reapplied her makeup an hour later, it struck her that this was the last time she'd ever sit in a dressing room, preparing for a show. Her life as a ballet dancer was taking its final curtain call after thirty years. Tonight's performance was sure to be emotional and stressful. She could feel the tears building up even now. Thank goodness no one knew her secret.

Malik returned just before the 'five minutes' call rang around the dressing room. 'Ready?' he asked, hugging her.

Suzette nodded. 'Thanks for everything, Malik. We will keep in touch after tonight, won't we?'

'Of course. We were good together, weren't we?' Malik said, releasing her and catching hold of her hands and looking at her seriously. 'You tell Pascal he'll have me to answer to if he ever hurts you.' He squeezed her hands. 'Ready?'

Suzette nodded and took a deep breath. Time to dance for Pascal.

* * *

Thunderous applause echoed around the theatre and camera flashlights dazzled as Suzette curtsied, taking curtain call after curtain call. A huge wave of adrenalin swept through her body. She'd done it. She knew without being told that tonight had been one of the best, if not the best, performances of her career.

Single-stemmed roses were flying onto

the stage from all directions as Malik appeared with several large bouquets, closely followed by the stage manager with another armful.

'This is unreal. You told people I was retiring, didn't you?' she whispered to Malik, accepting the flowers.

He nodded. 'Only this afternoon when you turned down my offer. Forgive me; I truly wanted you to go out on a high.'

Suzette reached up and kissed his cheek. 'I forgive you. This is amazing.'

'I think these are the flowers you will treasure though,' Malik said, handing her a bouquet of twenty-four white and pink lilies and pointing to the card nestling in amongst them. 'To my darling Evie. With all my love, Pascal.'

The stage manager handed her a microphone as she struggled to control her emotions and ushered her forward to the edge of the stage. Clutching her flowers, she looked in the direction of the box where she knew her friends were sitting and blew a kiss to them before addressing the audience.

'*Merci. Merci.* You have been a wonderful audience. *Merci* to all my fans for your loyal support down through the years.' Struggling to control the tears that were threatening to fall, she stood for ten seconds letting the atmosphere engulf her.

Sensing the curtains beginning to slowly close, she stepped back to allow them to pass in front of her.

Blowing one last kiss out over the footlights, she said, 'Tonight it's time for Suzette Shelby to say a final thank you — and goodbye.'

As the curtains closed, hiding her from view, she turned and walked towards the wings where she could see Pascal waiting for her.

Time to live Evie's life.

THE END

I'M WATCHING YOU

Susan Udy

Lauren Bradley lives a quiet life in her village flat, with only her cat for company. So why would anyone choose her as a target for stalking? As the harassment becomes increasingly disturbing, several possible candidates emerge. Could it be Lauren's old friend, Greg, who now wants more than just friendship? Sam, the shy man who works in the butcher's shop across the street and seems to know her daily routine? Or even handsome but ruthless Nicholas Jordan, her new boss to whom she is dangerously, but hopelessly, attracted?

FAIRLIGHTS

Jan Jones

The fortified pele tower of Fairlights, its beacon shining out across the harbour, has guarded Whitcliff for centuries. Sorcha Ravell thought she'd recruited the perfect restoration expert in Nick Marten — but he turns out to be dangerously attractive; knows more about her than she can account for; and is very, very angry. As the autumn storms build and the tension rises, Sorcha must overcome a paralysing physical fear and confront a terrifying mental enigma. What happened to her so many years ago? And why can she not remember?

DIFFICULT DECISIONS

Charlotte McFall

Tracy Stewart left the Derbyshire village of Eyam to pursue her dream of becoming a solicitor. Returning home for Christmas is the last thing she wants to do. A brush with Mike O'Neill starts to change her mind, but is it enough to make her stay? Mike has taken over running his father's bookshop, whilst working as a writer in secret. But can he keep his secret as well as the girl he loves?

TANGLED WEB

Pat Posner

After his beloved great-uncle has an angina attack, Jarrett tells his fiancée, Emily, that the elderly man's one wish is to live long enough to see him happily married. Emily agrees to bring their wedding forward but she's devastated when, on their honeymoon, she hears of a clause in Jarrett's great-uncle's will: the first baby boy born in the family will inherit the family business. Has Jarrett only married her so he can produce an heir before either of his brothers beat him to it?